Truth and Lies

Truth and Lies

Tamara Williams

James Lorimer & Company Ltd., Publishers
Toronto, 2002

First publication in the United States, 2002

James Lorimer & Company Ltd. acknowledges the support of the Ontario Arts Council. We acknowledge the support of the Government of Canada through the Book Publishing Industry Development Program (BPIDP) for our publishing activities. We acknowledge the support of the Canada Council for the Arts for our publishing program.

Cover illustration: Jeff Domm

Canada Cataloguing in Publication Data

Williams, Tamara L.
    Truth and lies

ISBN 1-55028-756-7

I. Title.

PS8595.I5632T78 2002   jC813'.54   C2002-900197-8
PZ7.W668275Tr 2002

James Lorimer   Distributed in the United States by:
& Company Ltd.,   Orca Book Publishers,
Publishers   P.O. Box 468
35 Britain Street   Custer, WA USA
Toronto, Ontario   98240-0468
M5A 1R7
www.lorimer.ca

Printed and bound in Canada

Chapter 1

I had a feeling that something wasn't right that morning. Maybe it was the way the trees were covered in wicked frost or perhaps it was the coldness of the night that made the walls creak and groan, registering their distress. It might have been the way my radio wouldn't tune into my favourite radio station. If it had, I might have heard the news. Not the way I would've wanted to hear it — but at least it wouldn't have been at school with everyone watching me, looking to see how I would react. Maybe it's crazy to think that if my toast hadn't burnt or the hydro hadn't gone off in the middle of the night, or if the batteries from my personal stereo hadn't died, that I might have been in a better mood, might have been in a better frame of mind to accept the horrible news. Instead, all I had to focus on during my walk to school were the strip malls, fast-food joints, and cheesy bars that littered south Oshawa.

I didn't see him coming or distinguish his truck from the masses headed to work. All of a sudden, this shadow loomed over me, then slush splashed all over my coat.

"Oh, great!" I shouted, jumping away from the onslaught of more mess on my clothes. Then I looked up and saw a familiar face grinning at me from behind the wheel of a battered 1984 GMC. My annoyance fell away and was replaced with a happy flutter as I opened the passenger's side and climbed in.

"Hey, babe! You shouldn't walk so close to the road," he said as he leaned over to give me a quick kiss before putting the truck into gear and heading toward the school. Jon Abbey, my boyfriend for the past six months. Tall, blond and, as far as I was concerned, the best-looking, sexiest guy at Oshawa Secondary. He was a year younger than me, but we would both graduate from school together in June. He was in the Tech stream — automotive, wood-working, and stuff; math and English weren't his best subjects — so it's amazing that we even met. Still, everyone knew him from the hockey team and he was someone who had a presence around the school.

"What time are you coming over tomorrow?" I asked. We always got together on Fridays.

"Oh, shit. I forgot tomorrow was Friday. I told Steve I'd go over to his place with the guys."

My stomach tightened. Jon's friends' favourite thing to do when they got together at Steve's was to drink beer and look at men's magazines. I hated it, but I didn't want to make a fuss and end up sounding insecure.

"Sorry, babe," he said patting my knee.

"Hey, no problem. Marcel and I have work to finish," I said lightly.

Jon snorted. And that was all he had to do to show his disgust with my gay friend. His attitude toward gays bugged me, but I'd learned to keep quiet about it. A lot of people aren't as tolerant as they should be. Jon was one of them.

As we pulled up in front of Oshawa Secondary, I said, "Give me a call," and stepped out of the truck. Then he was gone. I walked toward the school hitching up my coat ever so slightly, trying to keep the sludge off the edge of my dress. I'd read somewhere that a skirt trailing in mud was symbolic of something. I wasn't sure what, but I certainly didn't want the November grime clinging to me, sullying my clothes.

The sweet smell of marijuana wafted toward me from a large group huddled together — goths. I could never figure out if they all had naturally white, pasty skin or if they used some kind of makeup to make them look that way. What wasn't white was black — their eyes heavily outlined, black lips, hair dyed, fingernails painted, all-black clothes. Not my style of black but dramatic jackets, flared pants, clothes that were out of a vampire movie. Then there were the piercings and chains, everything to an extreme. Pierced eyebrows, chins, tongues, noses — and who knows what else? Their jewelry was all thick chains and leather. Some wore dog collars with studs, others had chains attached to their pants. I never could figure out if they dressed like that for shock value or whether they honestly enjoyed the look. I knew one thing for sure. They hated being called "Freaks," even though they called themselves that. Sometimes Jon got his kicks by riling a couple of the girls. I didn't know why he did it — maybe he was just looking for a reaction — but he loved getting this one girl all upset. He'd call her "Freak" and keep needling her until she blew her top and screamed at him. Last week she even pulled a knife on him outside the school, but Jon just laughed. Sometimes I wish he'd keep his opinions to himself.

Today, the smell of weed was pretty potent. I didn't know why the teachers at the school didn't do anything about illegal substances on school grounds. But I couldn't blame the problem on the teachers, like the media tried to do. After all, it wasn't their job to police the students. I just wished somebody would or could do something. A lot of us could use the help. I shifted my books and art portfolio from arm to arm — so much baggage I carried around with me. Too many things to do, too many places to go. I walked up the stairs of the school, careful to avoid ice patches so I wouldn't slip and make a fool of myself in front of everyone. I didn't care as much about what other people thought now that I was in OAC but, God, in grades nine and ten I was so insecure and anxious. "A neurotic twit" was what Jon called me. I used to think everyone was looking at my skinny, gangly body and laughing at me. But I wasn't imagining it. Kids did laugh at me — at lots of people — as a way, I've come to realize, to make themselves feel good. By creating misery in someone else, it somehow lifted them up and made them feel better. Thank God I wasn't in grade nine anymore. Still, every once in a while, those old feelings would creep in and torment me.

As I walked to my locker, I couldn't help but notice that there was a weird tone in the halls, an eerie quiet. I scrunched up my eyebrows and chalked it up to Oshawa — just one more thing I couldn't explain and didn't understand. I walked up the stairs and turned right through a set of doors into the English wing, then took another right. Locker number 2125. Red. The same locker I'd had since grade nine. It was a long walk to the art wing, but they had this new thing TAG or TAP — I could never remember because it kept changing — Teacher Advisory or something. It meant that instead of having our lockers with our own grade and our peers, we were mixed in with all the students in our TAP group. Once a month we met to discuss things like report cards and study skills — a big waste of time as far as I was concerned.

Opening my locker was an aesthetic experience. I treated my locker like it was a sanctuary, plastering the door and walls with prints of pieces by my favourite artists — Claudel, Hjerten, Van Gogh — clippings of exhibition openings, pictures of my own paintings and poetry. Poetry was my own subversive rebellion against the norm of my generation. I hated being like everyone else. I wanted to be an individual. People might think I was weird, but I didn't care.

As I shut my locker, Amy rushed over to me, eyes red and swollen like she'd been crying. Nothing unusual for Amy. She had been my best friend since kindergarten. She was the most emotional, sensitive person on the planet and at the drop of a hat could break into tears. You always had to be careful around Amy. She was like a fine piece of crystal sitting on the edge of a cabinet waiting to fall and shatter. But man, oh man — could she draw and paint! There was no doubt in my mind that of the two of us, she was the one sure to get into the Ontario College of Art and Design.

Lately Amy had started dating this Jesse guy who got on my nerves. Some heavy-duty Christian. Too prim and proper for my liking. It wasn't that I was jealous of his time with her — well, maybe a little. I used to be able to count on her to go downtown to the gallery with me or just hang out. Now I had to book her a week in advance, and even then she had to check in with Jesse.

I slung my arm around her shoulder, "Hey, Ames. What's wrong?"

Her look changed from sadness to fear. "You mean you haven't heard?"

"Heard what?"

She broke away from my embrace, staring at me in disbelief, then walked backwards saying, "I can't, Erin. I can't be the one."

My curiosity was provoked, but I just shrugged my shoulders, pegging it as Amy's usual overreaction to something. As I stepped into my homeroom, though, it was like walking into a funeral parlour — the room was hushed, and a couple of girls had their heads down on their desks and looked like they were crying. Marcel hadn't arrived yet, but that was nothing new. Three days out of five he was late, each time coming up with a very creative excuse.

We stood up as "O Canada" came on over the public address system, then the announcements. The same boring stuff as usual — basketball practice, yearbook committee, swimming club ... blah, blah, blah. Then there was a moment's hesitation before the principal coughed and said, "As you've probably heard on the news, one of our students, Marcel Lemieux ..." His voiced trailed off. What? What about Marcel? I turned my head around wildly, looking for someone who would explain, but no one would meet my eye. The principal resumed, "Marcel Lemieux is in critical condition in Oshawa General. He was found beaten last night on Bell Street, where it's believed he was out jogging. The police are on the case. If anyone has any information, please call Crime Stoppers ..."

I felt like I was going to suffocate, vomit and

faint all at the same time. I had to see him. I had to find out what had happened and who had done it. I needed answers — now. I picked up my stuff and ran out of the class. No one tried to stop me.

Chapter 2

After I heard the news about Marcel, I bolted from the school like a scared deer. I wandered the near-by streets aimlessly, trying to understand what had happened. I'm not sure how long I was out there — maybe fifteen minutes, maybe an hour. I think I must have been in a kind of shock, because I can't remember what I was thinking about and I don't think I even saw the houses and stores I was passing. No one stays in that state forever, though, and eventually I got myself together and decided I would walk to the hospital.

I've always hated hospitals. Not that I'm a wimp or anything. It's just that hospitals are reminders of places I don't want to be: institutions with borders and boundaries and padded walls. And sick people. I can take the blood and guts; it's the human frailty I hate and, of course, the fear — my own fear, the patients' fear, and that of their families.

By the time I finally reached Oshawa General,

I felt numb. I looked at the large, sprawling building. Marcel could be anywhere inside its walls. I finally found the reception desk in the lobby and asked the grandmotherly volunteer for directions.

"I'm here to visit Marcel Lemieux. Where do I go?"

She flipped through a binder.

"Lemieux, here it is. But it says, 'Only family.' Are you family?"

I lied, "Yes."

"Seventh floor, room 725."

I headed off to the banks of elevators. When I got up to the seventh floor, there seemed to be some sort of crisis happening. There was a knot of people in white coats standing around, arguing about something while buzzers were going off. I arrived just in time to hear a doctor order a nurse to get him something, lickety split. What a jerk. Did he think that, just because he was a doctor, he was God? That's one reason I never wanted to be a nurse like my mom — too many people telling me what to do. At least as an artist I would be my own boss; I would be in charge of my art.

I stood waiting at the nursing station, but no one paid any attention to me. Fine. I would just go and find Marcel's room. As I walked away from the station I could hear the same doctor chewing out another nurse. All these little dramas and meanwhile Marcel might be dying in a room somewhere on this floor.

Even though I had braced myself, I still wasn't

prepared for the sight of him lying broken in the hospital bed. I stood at the doorway and felt a cold shiver run over my body, like when I get out of a hot shower in the middle of winter. His disfigured body was hooked up to machines that were beeping rhythmically. Added to this was the drip, drip of the tube going up his nose. His right arm was in a cast and suspended over his head. His ribs looked like they were taped and his right leg was also in a cast. His face — the part I could see — was swollen and bruised beyond recognition. The rest was bandaged or covered in salve. As I stepped closer, I could see that his mouth was slightly caved in, like an old man who's taken out his dentures. That's when I started to bawl; they'd bashed in Marcel's teeth. Whoever had done this to Marcel must have really had it in for him.

Looks were so important to Marcel. He was fanatical about his appearance — body conscious and obsessive about his hair; even worse than Amy. Every day he asked me what I thought about his looks: was he too skinny? too fat? He was never satisfied with who he was and constantly changed his look to match some TV star or model he'd seen in one of the magazines he loved. His latest complaint was that he had too much hair; too much chest hair and way too much hair on his back. He wanted to look like the models in his magazines, androgynous with no body hair. As much as I tried to reassure him that he looked great the way he was — that his hairiness did not

11

make him look ugly, that he was gorgeous, hair and all — off he went to the salon to have it all waxed off. He said it hurt, but that he welcomed the pain as a necessary evil in order to achieve the perfect body.

As I looked at him now I thought, he's not going to be happy when he wakes up. If he wakes up.

A noise from the shadows of the room startled me, little whimperings almost like a kitten. In the corner was Marcel's mom, Lucie. She looked at me and tried to smile, but it was too much of an effort and she just sighed, the heaviness of her sadness weighing her down. Then she shook her head with a look of incomprehension.

I had known Lucie for ten years; ever since she and Marcel had moved into our neighbourhood and started going to our Catholic church. Right off the bat, my mom and Lucie hit it off because they were both French. I didn't pay much attention to Marcel — I had my own friends — but then he showed up in my grade two class barely able to speak English. Since I was the only one who understood him, I asked him to play with me at recess and walked home with him. We'd been buddies ever since.

Lucie was a small, fragile woman, with a large bosom. Marcel and his mom were close; they clung to each other as the only family they had in Ontario since the death of Marcel's dad four years earlier in a car accident. My mom and Lucie worked together at the same nursing home and were practically like sisters.

I wrapped my arms around Lucie's thin shoulders, "Je m'excuse. Je vais faire tout ce que je peux pour trouver ceux qui ont fait cela à Marcel."

"Merci, chérie." I gave her another stiff hug, feeling the bones through her blouse — sharp, jagged, skeletal. I could feel her body shake and quiver like a frightened rabbit. *Oh God*, I thought. *What am I going to do?*

I knew she probably didn't want to talk about it, but I had so many questions.

"What do the doctors say?" I asked.

She sighed deeply. "He's in a coma. They don't know if he will come out of it or not. He has two broken ribs, and —" She started to cry. "Erin, please find out who did this."

I felt the weight and responsibility of that request.

"I don't think Marcel had any enemies. Was he fighting with anyone lately?"

"Not that I know of."

"Did he run at the same time every day?"

"No, he wasn't that organized. Sometimes in the mornings, sometimes after school. Sometimes at night. Why did he have to choose that night?"

I had no answers to her question.

A nurse came in, all efficient, and took in the scene.

"No visitors. Just family," she said briskly.

I looked at Lucie, expecting her to come to my defence, to speak up on my behalf, but she didn't.

13

She just bowed her head, defeated, unwilling to talk back to those in charge, including the English nurse, the one she counted on to make her beloved son better. Obey the rules and everything will be fixed. I wanted to shake her, to tell her to stand up to the nurse — tell her that I was Marcel's best friend, that she knew me — that I was like family, that they could make an exception. But instead, Lucie offered a weak smile to me and quietly said, "I think you'd better go. Do what she says." I had too many feelings bubbling inside of me to think rationally, to think of some way to get around the rules. For now I would have to comply.

As I walked out of the hospital, the November wind hit me in the face like a slap. I breathed deeply, my lungs aching from the coldness and feeling my perspiration clinging to my back like cold ice. I was determined. I didn't care what I had to do to keep my promise to Madame Lemieux. I would find out who had attacked Marcel and they would pay for their crime.

Chapter 3

The next morning I woke up early and couldn't get back to sleep. I couldn't relax with the image of Marcel floating through my mind. I kept tossing and turning. Eventually, I just got up and threw on some jeans, a black turtleneck, and my leather jacket. At the last minute, I grabbed a pair of woollen mittens and a long scarf to cover my ears, knowing that with even these coverings I'd be cold in the November air.

It was six-thirty, and the street lights were still on. There was a stillness in the crisp air; it was almost peaceful, a word I never thought I'd associate with Oshawa. But the quiet stillness was soothing to the chaos inside my brain and I felt my head clear and my thoughts resolve, crystallize, as I walked past the mansions on Simcoe Street. I wondered if the night that Marcel had been beaten had been this quiet, this still. Had he felt a calm before the storm? The thought passed through my head that I was being dumb. If Marcel was beaten when he was out by himself, what was I doing walking alone? Part of me said, *Turn back, go back home.* Another part said, *If you give in, weaken, they, whoever they are, will have won.*

It was now seven, and the school doors by the gymnasium would be open. There was usually some team practising in the morning — volleyball, basketball. There weren't a whole lot of people at the school interested in sports, and the Oshawa Secondary teams were usually last at any championships, but I had to hand it to the coaches who stuck to it and kept the teams going instead of wimping out, getting discouraged.

As I opened the door, I expected to hear shouts and feet pounding the floor, bouncing balls, the usual sports-associated sounds, but the gym was silent and dark. Weird. As I walked down the corridor toward the art wing, the usual graffiti greeted me: *Long Live Freaks, Fuck the Pigs, Druids Rule.* I usually just ignored it, or at best admired somebody's creative artwork. I know that the administration tried to paint over the offensive words, but as soon as the walls were clean something new would appear. Today I noticed *Kill the Fags* in jagged black and red. I stopped and stared. Who wrote that? If the cops looked at it, would they come up with any clues? What about fingerprints? I made a mental note to mention it in the office.

Outside the art room, three lockers had been kicked in. I couldn't understand the senseless violence, the anger, that would make someone wreck school property, but I was starting to realize that I didn't understand a lot about humanity.

Mr. McPhaden had given me a key to the art room. I knew that if the principal or vice-principals found out, he'd be in big trouble — but I certainly wasn't going to tell. I put the key in the door and waited for the click, and then there was the welcome smell of the place I considered home away from home. I just wanted to be alone with the smell of paints, clay, turpentine, paper — all the things that stabilized me, made me feel whole, made me feel like the world wasn't a crazy place. I looked around at the art displayed in the room, our works in progress. Amy's watercolour stood on the easel, waiting for the last few finishing touches. I was always amazed at her ability to create an impressionistic world of colours melded into each other, wet on wet, and yet still keep her subject well defined. She loved water scenes and she'd often go by the river and try to capture the feel of nature. Yet beside that perfect beauty she had painted the juxtaposition of trash, shopping carts, used condoms, beer cans, and cigarette butts, all carelessly discarded. It was easy to do that to things, things that are actually garbage, but what about people? Are people so easily discarded? Beaten and then thrown to the side, waiting for a garbage truck or ambulance to pick them up, and put them in a place where people don't have to look at them, don't have to be reminded that this person is not like them. I thought of Marcel lying in bed, covered in bandages.

I glanced at the clock — seven-twenty. Ten more minutes and the vice-principals would be arriving. I could talk to them and see if anything was being done, if any suspects had been identified. I knew that they had given out the Crime Stoppers number. I seethed at the idea that they were treating this crime like any other petty problem that routinely was part of Oshawa Secondary — someone's Roots watch had been stolen, a teacher's car had been vandalized, someone's locker had been broken into — all crimes of cowards, people too scared to carry out their acts in front of others, hiding, pretending to be someone else.

I turned back toward Amy's watercolour and this time I noticed she'd made some subtle changes: the beauty of the river was far more prominent in the work and the garbage was less intrusive, less in your face, less a focus. The result was that the painting was not as powerful as she was capable of creating. The garbage was made to look almost decorative, pretty, a necessary component of the landscape, an acceptance that this indeed was what one found scattered beside rivers — it was just a part of life, something to be accepted. I wondered why she'd made the changes. I'd have to ask her when I saw her later.

Marcel's work stood next to hers. It was a bust of his dad. (I always thought the word *bust* was weird, but, hey, I didn't make up the English language.) Marcel was working from old pictures that he and his mom had, but personally I thought the sculpture was turning out to look way better than the person in the photograph. Marcel loved sculpture — clay, bronze, iron. Sometimes his work was representational; at other times his stuff was totally abstract.

I sighed. It was finally seven-thirty. As I got closer to the office I could hear a commotion, something more than just the usual morning greetings among the administration. There was panic. I opened the door and silence fell on the room. The four secretaries looked at me, their faces red. The two VPs were flushed, angry, anxious. No one said anything. I felt like a deer caught in headlights, staring at an oncoming car, an adversary. I was the enemy.

"May we help you, Erin?" It was the kind of question people ask politely to get you out of their hair, to send you on your way like a good little girl. I knew that I had to be brief, to the point.

"Have they found out who hurt Marcel?" I knew my voice sounded defensive, like I was anticipating the answer to be in the negative, but still I wasn't prepared for an attack. The answer was like a Rottweiler going for the jugular.

"Erin, everything is being done. We are not gods or supermen. Thankfully he wasn't killed. All is being done that can be done at this point. Now please leave."

"What? You're kicking me out of the school for asking a simple question?"

"Erin, get out. School is closed for the day."

"What do you mean?"

"There's been a bomb threat. Now leave."

At that moment a policewoman stepped forward, tall, confident, black. She held out her hand and shook mine with a firm grip. "Hi, my name's Dorothy Blake. We're doing all that we can for Marcel Lemieux, but our resources are spread so thin that it's difficult. Have a nice day off." She smiled, then turned back to the office personnel.

I turned and left, reluctantly. I hadn't even got to mention the graffiti I'd seen in the hall. Still, feelings of relief rushed through me. I was hopeful that this woman would find the people who were responsible.

Chapter 4

"Ames," I called to the figure ahead of me. The girl was slim with medium-length dark, wavy hair. I guess that would describe lots of the girls at my school, but the dead giveaway that it was Amy was her coat — her black thigh-length wool coat — and then of course her beret. Not the usual Oshawa choice of dress.

Amy had been heading toward the restaurant on the corner, but she turned when she heard my voice. So did the guy she was with — Jesse. They waited for me to catch up.

"What are you doing to do now that they're sending us home?" she asked.

"I don't know. Hang out or something. What are you up to?"

"We were just headed for a coffee. Wanna join us?" She smiled. I knew her invitation was genuine. The look on Jesse's face, though, was quite different. He didn't say a word, just stared at Amy in a way that made it clear he wanted to be alone with her. I'd seen that look tons of time on Jon, whenever I did something he didn't like.

Despite the scowl on Jesse's face, I had to admit, he was good looking — maybe even better looking than Jon. He was too clean-cut for me, but still a definite hunk, six feet or taller with spiky blond hair and clear skin. He dressed like a prep in expensive clothes. You didn't need to see the labels to know they were designer.

I thought of backing down — just going off and doing something on my own so I wouldn't intrude on whatever little tête-à-tête Jesse had planned — but then I thought, *Dammit, it's not like he owns Amy. She's my best friend and, besides, I feel like a coffee.*

We walked in uncomfortable silence to the coffee shop — nothing like a Starbucks or Second Cup, just a regular greasy spoon. The seats were fake leather, burgundy in colour. We could sit at a booth or on stools at the counter. The restaurant was right out of the fifties. The waitress took our order.

"How's Marcel?" Amy asked, trying to start a conversation that might interest all three of us. As Amy spoke, she put her hand over Jesse's — an act of tenderness, but also I think to make him feel more comfortable, more included.

"Not good. He's still in a coma and, when and if he gets out, there's going to be months of rehabilitation. The costs are going to be astronomical."

"Well, at least it's all covered."

"Not everything. Marcel's teeth were knocked in. The dental work won't be covered."

"Oh, you mean his mom will have to pay for that?"

Sometimes Amy could be dense. This was one of those moments.

"Yes," I said, trying to keep my voice patient. "The government only covers basic stuff, but if Marcel makes it, he's going to need a lot of help. Maybe plastic surgery and dental work. Lucie doesn't have a lot of private medical coverage. She's really scared."

"Oh." Amy looked embarrassed. "God. Who would do such an awful thing?"

"Some stupid homophobic idiot, that's who."

Jesse pulled his hand away from Amy's.

The coffee arrived. It felt good, the warm liquid flowing down my throat.

Jesse was visibly irritated. He was tapping his foot under the table and slurping his coffee, staring at the prints on the walls, then staring at the ceiling — anything not to enter the conversation.

"You can't be sure that Marcel was attacked because he was gay," Amy said after a minute. "Maybe it was just a random act of violence."

"I just know in my gut that someone singled him out deliberately. Whoever did it hates gays, and when the cops find the guy I hope they charge him to the limit!"

"I've had enough of this," Jesse said abruptly, slamming his cup down on the table. Coffee sloshed all over. "Did it ever occur to you that maybe he had it coming to him? That maybe he's being punished?"

"Punished?" I couldn't believe my ears. "How can you say something like that?" I asked, my voice bitter. "That's ridiculous."

"He's gay. He's a freak of nature. Maybe this is God's way of punishing him."

Amy looked like she was going to cry.

Maybe it was the look of incredulity on my face that pushed Jesse over the edge, but he stood up suddenly, grabbing his leather jacket. He turned to Amy. "You should choose your friends more carefully," he said. He obviously meant me.

Then he walked stiffly to the door, where he put on his jacket.

Amy looked frantic. She looked from me to Jesse's back.

"I gotta go, Erin," she said, jumping up. "Jesse, wait!"

I sat at the table, feeling all mixed up, a feeling I was getting used to — sad, angry, worried; worried especially about Amy and her involvement with this fundamentalist freak. But I knew that I could worry all day and, unless Amy chose to leave him, I was powerless, incapable of helping her, of telling her what I thought would be best for her. Besides, only she could decide that for herself.

Chapter 5

"Hey, watch it!" I said to the kid next to me. We'd been standing outside Ecstasy for an hour. It was ten o'clock and things were rocking. It was the same thing every Thursday — and on Friday and Saturday — at least an hour's wait and even then there was no guarantee of getting in. Jon and I were both underage. We each had fake IDs, which got us into most places unless they checked closely.

"I'm freezing," I said, stomping my feet and snuggling deeper under Jon's arm.

"Do you want my jacket, hon?" Jon asked, undoing the zipper, prepared to freeze for me. He was so sweet sometimes.

"You keep it on. Wrap me up." I snuggled in close to his chest, feeling warm, safe, and protected. A feeling I don't remember having since I was three. I loved the feel of Jon's cotton shirt against my cheek and the smell of his cologne — so manly, so reassuring.

So here I was, wrapped up like a cocoon. Couldn't see a thing. Could barely hear the sounds coming from the club or the people waiting in line with us, slowly inching their way forward. The most immediate sound was the beating of Jon's heart against my temple — safe and reassuring.

"Hey, man, need anything?" The voice was low, husky and the intent of the question was obvious.

"Nah, I'm okay," Jon said.

I felt myself relax. I hated it when he did drugs. I didn't mind smoking weed once in a while, but I'd tried ecstasy once and had had a bad trip. Jon and his friends, on the other hand, loved the stuff. I figured it was a phase Jon would grow out of, and I certainly wasn't going to nag him — something my mom used to do to Dad — and lose the best thing in my life.

A few minutes later, someone else came up to us, a guy I recognized from school. "Hey, Jon."

"Hey, man. What can I do for you?"

The boy didn't say anything, just cocked his head away from the lineup as if to indicate he wanted to talk to Jon in private.

"Uh, sure. Wait here for a minute, hon," Jon said, and the two of them walked off. I tried to see what they were doing, but they had disappeared around a corner. I stood alone in the lineup for several minutes.

At last Jon came back. "What was all that about?" I asked.

"Nothing, babe. Just something I had to sort

out, that's all." He put his arm around me and held me close as we shuffled toward the main entrance of the club.

"Brian and Jeff are supposed to meet us. Hope they're inside already."

I groaned inwardly — not those two. I thought Jon and I were out, just the two of us. Now I was going to have to share Jon with his friends. It's not like I minded him having friends. It's just that Jon was the kindest, sweetest guy when it was just the two of us, but with his friends he put on this macho act. He knew I hated it when he was like that, but he always said, "You don't want the guys to think I'm a wimp, do you?" He had a point there.

"Put on your nineteen-year-old face, hon," Jon said as we got close to the bouncers. There was a real knack to being nonchalant, to look like, *Of course I'm nineteen. How dare you question me!* There were about twenty people ahead of us. They looked like they were in some army — skinheads or neo-Nazis, I wasn't sure. I asked Jon.

"Nazis, of course. Look at the swastikas on their jackets."

Yeah. Like, duh, real observant. I had always thought that Nazis just hated Jews — but boy, oh boy, was I wrong! Nazis hated anyone they considered to be weaker than themselves or useless to society — the disabled, the elderly, the mentally challenged, and of course, gays.

I looked at the group in front of me. Could they

have beaten up Marcel? Did they just happen to find Marcel alone and vulnerable that night, and take the opportunity to demonstrate their hatred, to use Marcel as an example to all other gays in Oshawa to watch their backs? It was a possibility. Twelve of them with a hate-on could easily cause the damage that had been done.

Two more to go, then us. The Nazis got in, so I wasn't worried.

"ID?" The bouncer looked like he weighed three hundred pounds and was six-foot-four — a guy you wouldn't want to mess with.

We both flashed our pieces of paper, but he barely glanced at us before he waved us in.

Ecstasy was a world unto itself. Loud music, smoky darkness. A person could get high just breathing in the smoke around us. The place was jammed and really rocking. Jon looked over the crowd, searching for his friends. I held tightly to his hand like a kid not wanting to get lost in a department store.

"There they are." He started a path through the crowd, leading me. Jon has this presence, this don't-mess-with-me look. People just naturally parted to let us through. I liked that. I felt protected.

"Hey. So how's it going?"

The three of them high-fived each other; all the usual guy stuff. Brian and Jeff both said, "Hi, Erin" at the same time. Welcoming, friendly. Like, they knew they had to share Jon with me tonight. We sat at the small table, probably the only two seats left in the whole place. I noticed that Brian and Jeff were drinking water — so ecstasy was the drug of choice tonight. Shit.

* * *

When morning came, all I wanted was to shut off the sun and make the room dark, curl up in a little ball and forget about last night.

Everything was fine. Okay, everything had been fine — delicious, even — until about the third rum. Fine going down, but never coming up. I'd already made three trips to the bathroom. I just wanted the pain inside of me to go away. Some water, a couple of Tylenol, and two more hours of sleep would do it, but then I'd be late for school. Late for French and studying *L'étranger*. *The Outsider*. I could identify with Camus's main character, Merseult, who was distant, distracted, disconnected. That was how I'd felt looking at Marcel's tangled body — detached, like I was observing him from a distance.

It had been more than a week since Marcel had been attacked. Yesterday, I had gone to the hospital to visit him again. Looking at him in the bed, I couldn't help putting a frame around the scene, adding colours and splashes to the canvas — anger, hate, disgust. But then I was overcome with guilt when I realized I was making art out of Marcel's pain. Still, I knew Marcel would want me to paint my reactions, to take advantage of my muddled feelings, to make some sense of them on the canvas.

I drifted off and felt a story twist itself through my mind. Images from the previous evening — dancing, loud music. The guys admiring some girl's big breasts. Jon and I fighting. Then Dad walking away. I didn't see his face in the dream, but I knew that it was Dad — the only one who'd ever walked away from me and Mom. Then, just before I woke up, I dreamed that I caught Jon kissing someone in a dark corner. As I got closer I saw that the person he was kissing was a guy. I woke up crying.

"Ça va, ma chérie? Pourquoi pleures-tu?" my mom asked, shaking my shoulder gently. I didn't want my mom to know I was crying, that I'd been drinking. I didn't want to worry her. She had enough on her plate being a nurse and a single mom. I just wished that Mom had more of a life of her own, that I didn't have to feel so responsible for her happiness — but this is how things had been since I was four, since my father left us.

"Un cauchemar. Ça va," I said, forcing a smile. It was only a bad dream. I threw back the covers like I was thrilled to get up. "Je m'habille. I'll be dressed and ready in five minutes."

Choosing the colour of clothes to wear in the morning was never a problem for me, black, black, or black. Always crucial, however, to get the right combination: the black turtleneck with the black jeans was a serious student day; the black T-shirt with the hipster jeans was a more casual day; the black see-through blouse with the miniskirt was a sexy day. I wasn't into making any statements today, so I grabbed the cotton turtleneck and designer jeans. I hated being a slave to the fashion industry, to trends, but hey, I was a teenager. I wasn't about to make some political statement by wearing discount jeans or anything geeky like that.

I yawned and looked longingly at my bed. Why couldn't I have just twenty more minutes? I felt my head pounding and a terrible thirst. I pulled my jeans on over my hips and slipped on a sports bra before putting on my turtleneck. I didn't really need a bra, but it made things more comfortable on a cold day. Normally I was okay about the size of my breasts, but last night when Jon and his friends were ogling that girl, I'd wished there was something about me that would make Jon look at me in that way.

I stepped over a heap of dirty laundry — tangled socks, damp towels, jeans, skirts. An unpleasant odour, which I'd been trying to ignore for some time, wafted up from the pile. I couldn't quite ignore it, couldn't quite pretend that my room smelled like a rose garden. Besides dirty clothes, I could also smell paint. I glanced over at my easel where a half-finished canvas waited for finishing touches. There were splashes of red-pinks, slices of yellow, black outlines — creating images, forms, smooth lines, impressions. God, I was so unfocused these days! Couldn't keep my mind on anything. Couldn't concentrate. Couldn't think about anything but Marcel and finding his attackers. Then all of a sudden my focus melted and images of Jon entered my mind. Something wasn't right. Was my dream warning me that Jon was going to reject me? Then I thought about him kissing the guy in my dream. Yuck. What was that all about?

Geez, if I could just have one day alone, one day with my painting. And one day with the cops — maybe I could get everything sorted out, make everything the way it was supposed to be. I glanced at the prints on my wall — Pollock's *Lavender Mist*, Joan Mitchell's *Cross Section of a Bridge*, Frankenthaler's *Mountains and Sea* — such chaos. Splattering, spills, jagged lines. But all three of the prints spoke to me of the conflicted silence we all carry around within each of us. They showed exactly how I was feeling now — fragmented, swirling, twirling, all mixed up — yet from within the chaos one could sense a form, a coming together of all the senses. That's what I wanted to achieve in my work — a whole, a completeness. Only the painter knows for sure when something is finished, but the viewer can sense it.

"Erin!"

Shit! Just when I was gaining some clarity, just when I could've maybe sat down and finished that painting on my easel, just when, just when … Never enough time and then when I had it … always wasting it. I reluctantly closed the door to my bedroom, my haven, and grabbed my art portfolio and backpack full of the homework that I hadn't done last night.

I stumbled down the apartment staircase, trying to put on my black leather coat while chowing down a nutrition bar. The first blast of frozen air was perfect medicine for a hangover. I threw my bags into the back seat of Mom's car and slid into the passenger side beside her.

"You look horrible" was her first comment to me.

I slouched in my seat, fastened my seat belt, and closed my eyes, willing the Tylenol to take effect.

"What time did you get in last night?"

"I dunno. Midnight." Midnight was my curfew.

"I was awake at midnight, and one, and two — and you still weren't home." A pause and then, "I worry about you, honey."

Great. Now the guilt trip. But thankfully she changed the subject.

"How's Marcel?"

"Not good. Still in critical condition."

"Have they caught those horrible people yet?"

"No."

"Do they have any suspects?"

"I don't know, but I'm going to ask. When we were standing outside the club last night, I overheard one of the Nazis talking."

"Are Nazis and skinheads the same?"

"Apparently not."

We rode in silence a few more minutes, then it was like someone had flipped a switch in my mom's head.

"Erin, you're not getting involved in this, are you? You have to let the police handle it."

"If I did that, nothing would get done. I promised Lucie that I would find out who did this, and I plan to keep my promise."

"Erin, you don't have time. This is your OAC year. What about college? Scholarships?"

"Dad said ..."

"You know that your father makes many promises he can't keep."

I breathed deeply, trying not to freak out. All this pressure. I couldn't take it. My head pounded. I closed my eyes, but then things started to spin around — not good. *Open them fast*, I told myself.

Up ahead, I saw the school with the usual stragglers outside. Mom stopped the car and I got out.

"What time will you be home tonight?"

"Midnight. Jon and I are going out."

My mom's face tightened. I knew that she wasn't keen about all the time I spent with Jon, but she chose not to make an issue about it.

"No later."

"Okay, Mom. Love ya."

Then she was gone.

Chapter 6

"Get your fucking hands off me! I didn't do it."

Two cops dressed in neatly pressed uniforms escorted a neo-Nazi to a cruiser parked in the front of the school.

"What's going on?" I asked the closest student to me, a short grade niner.

"Guy's busted."

"For what?"

"Beating that gay kid."

"Marcel Lemieux?"

"Yeah, whatever."

"How did they find out?"

"Someone ratted on him."

"Do they have any evidence?"

The kid looked at me with this are-you-real look, then asked, "Are you some kind of cop?"

"No, just interested."

He backed away with a scowl on his face.

Well, at least I'd found out the basics. I took

one last look at the kid in the back of the cop car. I couldn't hear him, but by the contortions on his face, it was obvious that he was furious. Relief flooded through me, knowing that someone had been caught, something had been done. I wasn't surprised it was the neo-Nazis, and no one else would be either. Everyone knew they were responsible for the break and enter at the school last year. It would be hard not to know when they'd been stupid enough to leave swastikas spray-painted on the side of the building. I knew I shouldn't make assumptions and blame someone without having all the facts — but if someone chooses to be part of a visible group, a gang really, I'd say that person is a fair suspect.

I was so lost in thought, I almost missed the small piece of paper stuck in the upper slot of my locker. It fluttered down when I reached to the top shelf for my English text. I figured it was Amy asking me to meet her after school or to have a nice day — she was into random acts of kindness these days. When I glanced at the writing, though, it wasn't Amy's usual scrawl. Instead, the message was written in black block capital letters. STOP ASKING SO MANY QUESTIONS OR YOU'LL BE NEXT. I laughed, thinking it must be a joke. It wasn't Amy's style, but nothing else made sense. I stuffed the note into my backpack and rushed to homeroom.

I had all these muddled feelings — elation, relief, amusement — but above all else a huge hangover. There had been a bit too much stimulation for one morning.

Mr. Galaghan had just started his lecture on Virginia Woolf and stream of consciousness writing — really cool stuff — when the tranquil, civilized classroom environment was shattered by the shrill ringing of the fire alarm. Not again! Some idiot pulling the alarm as a prank, showing off to friends, watching the whole school respond to this one action. I was sick of these interruptions. We all stood up, gathered our books and shuffled out of the door. A teacher at the end of the hall was yelling, "Hurry up, let's get going! No stopping at your lockers!"

Shut up, I thought to myself. *We're going, we're going.* I hated teachers — or anybody for that matter — using situations to assert their power, to make themselves feel puffed up.

"Hey, Erin, wait up!" a voice shouted at me. I turned and saw Amy waving at me from amidst the tide of the hundreds of students pushing against me like a herd of cattle steadfastly walking to the slaughter. Someone's sack pushed roughly into me.

"Watch where you're going!" I said to the unknown student, who proceeded to turn around, curl his lip, and scowl. I stood with a level gaze — never, ever, show weakness — especially at this high school. Especially in Oshawa.

"Hey, Erin. How's it going?" Amy asked, putting her arm around my shoulder.

"Rotten!"

"Late night?"

"Yeah. Jon and his friends and I were at Ecstasy."

"I thought you decided not to go there on week-day nights."

"Yeah, well so much for that decision."

Amy sort of looked at me with an expression of concern, but I thought I detected more than that, almost a judgment, a disapproval that was not at all usual for my buddy Amy.

"How are things between—"

We followed the line, the masses, out of the school onto the sidewalk. A teacher was yelling, "Move along, move along."

It was freezing. Ames and I tried to talk, but our frozen lips interfered with the possibility of any intelligent conversation.

"What a bummer," Amy mumbled. "We were right in the middle of writing a test. Now I'll have to spend another night remembering all those dates and stuff. One prank a week is enough. Don't these kids ever get bored?"

I looked at my watch. Five after ten. I should've stayed in bed — a lot of good this morning was amounting to. Thankfully, I had my backpack and some books. Then I remembered the note.

"Hey, Ames. I got your message. Nice joke!"

She looked at me with a puzzled expression.

"Nice acting. But I know it was you."

"Sorry to disappoint you, Erin, but I haven't a

clue what you're talking about."

"Hey, you're good. Have you been studying drama on the side?"

"Erin, I don't know what you're talking about." The abruptness of her tone told me that she wasn't kidding.

"So you didn't put this in my locker?" I pulled out the slip of paper and showed it to her.

She read it, then said, "Erin, you need to take this seriously. Show it to the police and keep your nose out of the whole mess."

I was really getting irritated with her. I hated being lectured to, even by my best friend.

"You're probably right. But I don't have to think about that anymore since they caught the jerk! I'm outta here. Want to come with me?"

"Where are you going?"

"To the hospital, of course." I couldn't help being irritated. Everyone was acting like Marcel had ceased to exist. "I want to tell Lucie the good news that they've caught the guy."

Amy looked down at her feet.

"Uh, Erin, I heard they're going to have to let the neo-Nazi go. Not enough evidence."

"What! How can it be? It's so obvious that, even if it's not him, it's one of his friends."

"Apparently they were all at the same party that night on the other side of town."

"Then who could have done it?" I was shouting now.

"Erin, isn't it good enough that Marcel is alive

39

and getting better? Why can't you let go of this obsession of knowing who did it? Let the police look after it."

I looked at Amy like she had three heads. How could she be so callous? How could she not care or want to know the truth? At that precise moment I felt a horrible feeling inside of me — something like hate — and I felt like slapping her.

Then she turned conciliatory.

"Come on, Erin, they'll find out who did it. You know at this school people can't keep their mouths shut for too long."

I realized that she was right. My hostility was not going to help get anything solved.

"Why don't we go for a cappuccino and then visit Marcel?"

I couldn't argue with that suggestion.

Chapter 7

I love the smell of freshly brewed coffee, the idea of sitting around a small table discussing ideas. It seems so civilized, so adult. Something I imagine Parisiennes doing every day.

Amy ordered a mochaccino — chocolate and coffee mixed together with loads of whipped cream and caramel sauce on top. I just stuck to my regular cappuccino.

The coffee shop was empty except for a guy by the window reading the paper. Must be nice to be able to come in here — not to have to go to school or work — just order your favourite deluxe coffee and read. But maybe you'd get bored with it after a while.

Amy and I chose a spot at the back of the café. Dark, yet cozy, with its eclectic decor from the fifties. Amy's cheeks were rosy. Her eyes sparkled. I hadn't seen her look so radiant in ages. It didn't take a rocket scientist to figure out what was up.

"How are things with Jesse?" I asked, knowing the answer before she opened her mouth.

"Wonderful." She smiled and wrapped her hands around her mug in a contented sort of way, and then sighed.

"Why don't I ever see you out anymore?" I asked. "Parties? Dances? What's going on?"

"Jesse's parents don't let him go to dances or anywhere where there might be questionable substances. You know — alcohol, drugs."

"What's their problem?"

"They belong to this church with really strict rules."

A shiver went through my body, like an ominous warning. "So you're telling me that this church dictates its members' behaviour?"

"Well, it's not like that exactly. It's more like explaining the right way to live as outlined in the Bible."

"So it's not a cult?"

"No, no." She laughed. "It's just a regular church that believes in a literal translation of the Bible."

"What if the Bible's not right?"

Amy started to look peeved. "Look, Erin. I'm not asking you to agree or believe any of this. Why can't you just be happy for me for a change?"

"I'm happy that you're happy. I just don't feel like I know Jesse very well, and I miss having my best buddy around."

She relaxed noticeably and took a sip of her coffee, leaving a whipped cream mustache on her upper lip. I smiled and motioned with my own napkin. She laughed and wiped it off.

"So tell me more about Jesse."

"Well, he's the greatest guy. He's really, really smart. And he's good-looking, don't you think?"

I shrugged. It was hard to deny he was handsome.

"Not to mention, he kisses pretty good too."

"Sounds like a real catch. We should all get together and do stuff. You and Jesse and Jon and I."

Amy fidgeted on her seat, looking uncomfortable and then coughed. "I'd like to. It's … it's …"

"It's what, Amy?"

"It's just that Jesse tends to like to hang around people from his church."

"What are the rest of us going to do? Contaminate him?"

"It's just something they have about being separate."

"I'm sorry, Amy. This is just too weird for me. Like, this is the twenty-first century. I can respect his belief in the Bible and all that, but he sounds like a fanatic. You know what religious fanatics are capable of."

"It's not like that at all. I'm just coming to understand that some things are right and some things are wrong, and if we choose to avoid the wrongs we're — you know — ultimately better for it."

I sipped my coffee and thought a bit more. Then as if a flash of light had hit me, I suddenly remembered our last conversation with Jesse.

"So what do Jesse and his church think about gays?"

Amy coughed and her face went red. She stared into her coffee, not answering.

"Well?" I pushed.

"They believe that homosexuality is wrong. They believe that AIDS is God's judgment on those who choose to disobey His laws."

"Listen to yourself, Amy! Do you agree with that? What you're saying — it's not exactly compassionate, is it? Shouldn't religious people love everyone — even people they don't agree with?"

"Well, yeah. I've thought of that a couple of times."

"So Jesse thinks it was the hand of God at work when Marcel got beaten up? God's will?"

Amy shrugged halfheartedly.

I scrunched my eyes together, trying to make some logical sense out of what my friend was telling me.

"Does God sometimes use people to carry out his plans?" I asked.

"I don't know. I guess."

"So somebody like Jesse would feel that they were doing God's will by beating up Marcel?"

"Erin, I know what you're suggesting and you're all wrong. Jesse and his friends would never hurt anyone."

"Okay, okay." I was willing to drop it for now, but I'd just added a new suspect to my list.

As we were leaving, two rough-looking guys in leather jackets walked in. I had heard some members of The Apocalypse had moved into the area. Was that who these guys were? I was glad to get away from them. They gave me the creeps.

We walked in silence to the hospital and up the elevator to Marcel's floor, each of us lost in our own thoughts.

Nothing had changed in Marcel's room since I was last there. The same tubes, the same monitors, the same bashed-in face. I was more prepared to see Marcel now, but it still drove me crazy to think of the brutality he had experienced, the idea that someone had left him on the street to die.

Lucie rose from her seat.

"Have you been home?" I asked in French.

She looked uneasy. "Just to pick up clothes, mail, answer messages."

I stepped over and hugged her — enveloping her in my embrace like she was a child. She clung to me.

"Would you like a coffee?"

"That would be nice … but I didn't bring …"

"No problem."

I reached into my pocket and pulled out two toonies.

"Ames, the machine is down the hall to the right. Sugar and cream, right?"

"Merci, mon enfant. Sit, sit." Lucie motioned toward the only chair in the room. "My legs need the exercise."

But I could tell by the way she pulled herself across the floor that she was exhausted. I took her by the elbow and guided her to the chair. She sat down and breathed a heavy sigh.

"Have the police been in today?"

Lucie looked distractedly at the beeps on the monitor.

"Lucie," I repeated, "have—"

"No, no, not today. They went to the house and looked around Marcel's room for some — how do you say — *indices*?"

"Clues," I answered.

"Yes, yes. That's right. Clues."

"And did they find anything?"

"An address book full of phone numbers of people I'd never heard of, a diary, and … and …" her voice cracked, "some marijuana."

Lucie pointed to some books on the table. "There are the things the police found. They asked me to look through and see if I recognized any names — people who might have wanted to hurt Marcel — but I don't know many of his friends. Just you. Maybe you might recognize someone."

She pointed to Marcel's diary. "Take that too. I don't think Marcel would want me to read that."

I picked up the spiral-bound notebook covered with magazine pictures — mostly good-looking men — logos from that alternative magazine *Adbusters*, and his own drawings and scribbles. I flipped through the notebook, wondering if Marcel would want even me to look at this — a diary is a private thing, something I wouldn't want any of my friends to ever read. Still, this was a special case. This was Marcel's life, and I knew he'd want me to find the person who had attacked him.

At that moment Amy came back in with the cup of coffee and two Cokes. I smiled at her, trying to put her at ease. It was obvious she didn't want to be here, didn't want to be entangled in this. She wanted to help, but she was uncomfortable around sickness, around Lucie's sorrow. I figured it would be best if we left for now.

I put Lucie's coffee down on the bedside table and gave her a big hug. "I'll be back tomorrow. I'll read through these," I said, pointing to the address book and diary. "I'll let you know if I discover anything."

"Thank you," she said, sipping the coffee.

I put my hand on Amy's elbow and guided her out of the room. Once out in the hall she was visibly more relaxed. She handed me one of the Cokes, opened hers, and took a long swig.

"Boy, what a mess! I thought he'd look better than that."

"They did quite a job. That's why I have to find out who did it."

"Leave it to the cops, Erin. You can't do it on your own."

She was starting to sound like a broken record. I tried to keep my voice level. "I know, but this is something I have to do."

"Yes, ma'am. We know that when you set your

mind to something there is no changing it. You're such a mule."

She smiled as she said it, and I gave her a little punch on the arm.

The exit doors slid apart as soon as we stepped onto the mat. I felt my body go rigid from the cold, making me feel vulnerable, pointing out my weaknesses, my fears, the way the whole situation intimidated me. I guess I wasn't as strong as I pretended to be. We walked past the boxes of newspapers. I was shocked to read the headlines of three of the leading papers. "Boy Beaten." I stepped closer.

"Hey, Ames, they've finally picked up on Marcel's story." I walked toward the boxes. Hope and relief that something was finally going to be done flooded through me. It didn't take me long to discover that it wasn't Marcel they were writing about at all.

Thirteen-year-old beaten outside his private school. Community up in arms. Parents offering a reward.

I slipped a loonie into the slot and pulled out a paper. I couldn't believe my eyes. It was almost an identical type of beating, leaving the victim in critical condition at Sick Kids Hospital. The attack was believed to be racially motivated. Skinheads had been seen around the schoolyard for some time.

"Come on, Erin. Bring it home, I'm freezing," Amy urged.

"I can't believe this. I just can't believe it."

"That someone else got beaten up?"

"No! The coverage! It's the same crime. The same situation. Marcel's beating made it to page ten as a token story in the *Oshawa Times*. This is on the front page of every paper."

"Maybe it's because the kid is only thirteen."

I looked at Amy sideways, trying to decide whether she was kidding or really believed that. Amy could be so naive at times.

"The reason this kid's beating is getting coverage is because his parents are rich and his community is affluent." I tried to be patient as I explained. "Things like this aren't supposed to happen in *good* neighbourhoods in Toronto. Only in places like Oshawa."

Amy looked perplexed. "Do you really think so? That would be wrong."

"Exactly. That's why I have to do something."

Chapter 8

I needed to be alone to sort through my thoughts. "Amy, I've got some homework to do, so I'm gonna split."

"Me too. I want to be home for Jesse."

We gave each other a quick hug and then I turned west and she east. After a few moments, I turned around and watched her walk away from me. I was thinking about everything she'd just told me about Jesse. Jesse's dogmatic fanaticism and his growing influence on Amy scared me. I didn't know if someone with those beliefs would take them to such an extreme that he'd hurt another person. But after the terrorist attack in the United States on September 11, 2001, I knew that anything was possible.

Amy turned left, heading north on Simcoe. I shook my head to try to clear it. There were too many thoughts, too many worries swirling around in it. Then thoughts of the newspaper article surfaced, and I felt anger grip me. I grabbed the paper, ready to rip it into little pieces, to destroy the words of inequality, unfairness — even if it was only one paper out of thousands. At the last moment, though, I stopped myself. I had come up with a plan. I slipped the newspaper into my backpack and headed south to the Oshawa Art Gallery.

The day was still grey but warming up, as I made my way south, past stores and restaurants. Words were beginning to form in my mind as I organized all my concerns. Four guys on motorcycles roared by, momentarily disrupting my thoughts. Then they were gone. I passed a beautiful church with ornate stonework, a high steeple, stained-glass windows. I must've passed the church a thousand times — rushing to school, to band practice, to Jon — and all this time I had missed this beautiful structure in the middle of Oshawa. The sun peeked out over a cloud and just a glimmer appeared, just a little shine but enough to brighten and highlight the brilliant stained glass on the east side of the church. I marvelled at the detailed work and the myriad of colours — purples, blues, and yellows. I felt a wave of peace flow through me like a rippling brook, and in me rose a hope that things might work out. That things *would* work out. I tore my gaze away from the church, promising myself to return when I had time to sketch.

I waited to cross the street, then rushed across the three lanes of traffic and headed inside the Art

Gallery. I knew what I had to do. I had to write a letter to the editor of a newspaper, and I had to do it while my resolve and my reasons were burning inside of me. The Gallery's coffee shop would be a perfect place to compose the letter. Then, as a treat, I would allow myself to look around the Gallery — see what was new, look at my old favourites.

The coffee shop was quiet. There were two elderly women sipping tea in the corner. The one waitress was neatly dressed in a straight black skirt and a plain white blouse. She had her hair pulled back and, when she saw me come in, she smiled in a friendly, welcoming way. But behind that smile I could detect weariness and sadness, and for a brief moment I thought about my mom.

"Could I get a coffee, please?"

"Sure thing. Anything to eat?"

I glanced over at the glass showcase filled with expensive deserts and was tempted, then spotted a tray of muffins covered in glass.

"A muffin, please."

I sat down at the small table, laying my jacket on the back of the chair. I could feel the dull ache behind my left eye beginning to throb. Hangover. Migraine. What I really wanted to do was to crawl back into bed. But not yet, not until I had done something worthwhile that day.

By the time the woman brought me my coffee and muffin, I had my papers and pen set out in front of me. The crumpled newspaper's front page was spread out. I cleared a place for her to set things down.

I nibbled on the muffin — lemon poppy seed — savouring the tartness of the lemon and the grittiness of the seeds.

The waitress glanced at the paper as she set down the milk. "What's the world coming to, eh? First that kid in Oshawa. Then this. I've got two little ones and I worry sick about them. I can't be with them all the time to protect them from the wackos out there."

"How old are your kids?" I asked, trying to be polite.

"Five and seven."

"A boy and a girl?" I guessed.

"Yeah, the boy's the oldest. Just like his Dad. But it's the little one — Jeanie — that I'm worried about. Only five and already interested in lipstick and Britney Spears, stuff she sees on the television while at the sitter's." She shook her head. "I'll leave you to yourself."

The coffee was strong and comforting. The blank paper stared up at me and my pen stood poised to write what needed to be written. But, just like the moment when I stand in front of an empty canvas and my mind goes blank and fear almost consumes me, I felt doubts and questions creeping up. I knew that I had to get started, write anything or I'd lose my courage. I began by jotting down the key ideas I wanted to express: about social classes, about valuing human life based on wealth, about a privileged elite, the idea that a crime is a crime. Within a few minutes my pen was flying. Words, sentences, arguments. In a half an hour I had written five pages of rough draft. The first draft was always the hardest part for me. Now I just had to take it home and polish it, and make sure that I had presented my ideas in a fair and rational way, not as an emotional tirade.

I sat back in my seat and blew out a deep breath. I glanced over at the waitress. I was ready for another cup of coffee. She was serving two women in suits — they looked like bankers or librarians. A couple sat down in the place where the two older women had been. I hadn't even seen them leave or the new people come in.

"Another cup of coffee?" the waitress asked, the pot held in her right hand while her left hand held the small plastic milk containers.

"Sure."

"I would've asked sooner, but you seemed to be pretty serious about your work. I didn't want to interrupt."

"Thank you." I smiled.

"Are you a reporter or something?"

"I'm not a reporter, but I'm writing a letter to the paper. To the editor."

"About that kid?" She pointed to the paper on the left-hand corner of the table.

"Kind of." I didn't feel like getting into details. The ideas were still fresh and I didn't want to hamper their strength by talking. "The guy you mentioned that was beaten last week in Oshawa was my friend."

Her eyebrows went up.

I finished my coffee, gathered up my stuff, and left a tip for the waitress. Now for the Gallery. I flashed my pass at the security guard. He nodded as I entered, recognizing me as a regular. This week a Toronto painter was on display — Kazuo Nakamura, one of the two surviving members of the Painters Eleven, a group of vanguard abstractionists active in the fifties. It was abstract expressionism — my favourite, but a style that seemed passé to some in the twenty-first century.

Then I saw it at the end of the room. The hotness of the blue was the first thing to capture my eye, and as I got closer, I became mesmerized by the indigo strokes, the intertwining latticework. I stood and gazed for at least ten minutes until my back started to ache and my legs got sore. I finally tore myself away from *Inner View* to look at the other canvases: *Pascal's Triangle*, too mathematical for my liking; *Trees, in Forest*, a softer yet early presentation of reality; and then *Structures and Fractals*. I was intrigued by the contrast of the more mathematical pieces and the abstract. I must've spent at least an hour in that room going back and forth, painting to painting, my eyes always wanting to return to the blue abstract. I felt invigorated and inspired, and I was eager to get back to work on my own pieces.

Before I left, I thought I'd take a quick look around the sculpture gallery. There was a special exhibit — really cool stuff. Sculpture was not my forte, but I'd have to include some three-dimensional pieces in my Ontario College of Art and Design application, and I thought I might get some inspiration looking at the new pieces.

The Gallery was quiet as usual, almost empty. So when I entered the sculpture gallery, I was startled to see a guy standing in front of one of the male nudes. It took me a few seconds to realize that this was not just any guy, any art observer. It was Jon. Jon, the same guy who had refused to attend a show of Robert Mapplethorpe's photographs a couple months ago, who had dismissed his work as disgusting, done by a fag. We'd had a huge fight about it. And yet here he was, standing in this room, observing subject matter he apparently hated. I couldn't handle it. I didn't know what to say, what to do. So I turned quietly and headed for the exit. As soon as I got outside, I broke into a run, trying to chase the confusion out of my head.

Chapter 9

"Mom?" I called out, but felt the emptiness of the apartment.

I slipped off my black shoes — damp from the outdoor slush — feeling my wet toes and the discomfort of wet socks. I pulled those off, too, and headed for the kitchen. I plugged in the kettle and then set my stuff on the kitchen table, feeling the inevitable weight of my thoughts coming colliding in. I knew that I would have to think about what I saw at the museum — that I couldn't just ignore what I'd seen — but what should I do?

It just didn't make sense. Jon avoided museums, or anything to do with exhibitions. At first, I thought that he just felt uncomfortable about art. Then I started to realize that Jon just wasn't interested in anything I was interested in. In fact, it seemed that he purposely put down the things that were important to me. I'd tried to talk to him about my work and why I valued it so much, but he would just shut down and say that he didn't want to talk about it.

What was wrong with me? Why did I like someone like this, anyway?

The kettle's whistle blew and I roused myself from the kitchen table. The china teapot sat in the dish drainer, drip drying from Mom's morning tea. I grabbed my favourite mug, the one with a reproduction of Tom Thomson's *The Jack Pine* on the side. It had chips around the edges and the colour was starting to fade, but it still made me feel special. I'd always thought that feeling came from the beauty of the painting on the mug, but as I settled back at the kitchen table, my hands wrapped around the warm mug, I thought maybe it had more to do with the fact that it was one of the few things my dad had given to me.

What made me think of that? Because it was November and getting closer to Christmas, the time I could count on good old dad to try and fit in a visit between looking after his lovely trophy wife and their beautiful house and their perfect lives? It made my stomach churn just thinking about him — his lies, his deception, how he hurt Mom. How he walked out on us.

Positive. Gotta think positive, I said to myself. Chase those nasty Dad thoughts away. I breathed in deeply, holding the air in my lungs, then breathed out, making my lips vibrate as the air passed over them. Mom had taught me that. She said it was something women were taught when they were in labour. She said that the oxygen calmed the nervous system and the lips thing was a distraction from the pain. Yep, she was right, and I smiled thinking about my mom and her quirky ways. She was as thin as a bean pole, but full of energy. She could never sit still, always had to have a project on the go. I glanced around at the living room; a testament to her busyness. Knitted throw rugs, handstitched quilts, needlepoint samplers, dried flower arrangements. I never really thought about it, but Mom's craftiness was really a form of art, a form of creating beauty. As I realized how comfortable she made this apartment with her crafts, I was grateful for her effort to make it into a home for us — no matter how sad and lonely she must feel at times.

A key turned in the lock, and Mom pushed the door open with her shoulder. Her arms were laden with grocery bags.

"Hon, can you get the two bags in the hallway?"

I fetched the sacks, closing the door as I brought them inside.

"It's sure getting to be like winter out there," she said making her way to the kitchen and already beginning to unpack. "How was your day, honey?"

"Oh, the usual. Fire alarm."

"Again?" She poked her head around the corner to see if I was kidding.

"I'm serious." I suddenly remembered my letter to the newspaper. "Hey! I have something I want to show you."

I pulled the letter from my backpack and handed

it to her. She came to the table with her own mug. I poured her a cup of tea and watched her face as she read.

I wasn't really expecting anything from her — approval or disapproval. She was usually okay about most things I did, even if she was concerned. That's the nice thing with Mom and me — we've got trust.

Her brow furrowed as she read slowly, sipping on her tea. When she was finished, she set the letter down and stared out the window, then turned back to me with a soft smile.

"Well written, honey. It reminds me of my university days in Quebec when we protested and went on strike." She sighed, "Such idealism. I miss those days. Your father and I ..." Her voice trailed off. I knew that she was thinking about Dad.

"Well, the son-of-a-bitch is gone. Why waste your time thinking about Dad?"

"Don't talk about your father like that. He's a good man!"

"A good man leaves his family for the woman next door?"

"Feelings change. I knew that he didn't mean to hurt me or you, but he felt that Linda was his destiny, his salvation."

"Sounds pathetic to me."

"Well, it is. He was a very messed-up man. He didn't know himself. I still don't know if he does. But I think he felt that being with Linda would end his confusion and help him get a grip on life."

"Sounds pretty lame."

"But it happens all the time to men and women. People look to a relationship to define themselves." She looked pointedly at me for a minute, and I didn't know what she was getting at. Then it hit me. She was talking about Jon and me.

"It's not like that with Jon and me." I started to feel my back go rigid.

"Okay," she said, then went back to her tea. I knew that she wasn't convinced

"So where are you going to send this?"

"The *Globe and Mail*, the *Star* and the *National Post*. See if any of them will publish it."

"You're better off e-mailing. It's faster and gets directly to the editorial staff. Besides you want the letter to have an impact when the news is fresh."

"Great idea. I'll send it right now." I picked up my backpack and headed to my room. The hallway was lined with family pictures from happy times. I wished Mom would get rid of the ones with Dad, though.

I quickly got down to work at the computer and typed up the letter. After a quick spell and grammar check, it was ready to send. I had the e-mail addresses for the *Globe* and the *National Post*. I'd just have to find the *Star*'s. Maybe Jon had a paper at home. I pressed Send and then waited for my Internet connection to go down before calling Jon. We could only afford one phone line.

I dialled Jon's number with a sick apprehension in my stomach, unsure whether I should mention seeing him at the Gallery.

"Yo!" His usual greeting.

"Hey, it's me. What did you do today?"

"Nothing much. Split after the fire alarm. Hung out with the guys, shooting pool."

"All day?"

"You know those guys. Once they start playing, they lose all track of time."

"Yeah." I felt the knot in my stomach grow bigger and my throat tighten. He was lying. What was he trying to hide? What was going on? I felt like confronting him with the truth, but something held me back, saying, *Wait. You'll find out when the time is right.*

"Yo, earth to Erin. Comment ça va?"

I smiled. I loved it when he tried to speak French.

"Sorry, I was lost in thought."

"What are you up to?"

"Actually, writing a letter to the newspapers. I've e-mailed a copy to the *Globe* and the *Post*. I wondered if you had a *Star* lying around and could give me the e-mail address."

"Let me check."

He set the phone down, and I could hear the familiar voice of Carrie, his younger sister, asking him what he was doing. Then he was back.

"Sure, here it is." He read the address over the phone. "What's this all about?"

"Oh, I'm just writing to the editors to point out the disparity in their coverage of Marcel's beating and the rich kid's story."

"Erin, why can't you leave it alone?" There was

something in his tone that irritated me. I had to go before I said something I'd regret later.

"See ya at school tomorrow."

"Yeah. Bye."

Once those letters were taken care of I could focus on my homework. As I pulled my books out of my bag, Marcel's diary fell to the ground. I'd forgotten I had it. I knew that I should probably take it to the police. It might have evidence in it, after all. But I was curious, interested myself. I knew that if Marcel wanted anyone to read his diary, it would be me. So I propped up my pillows and sat back on the bed. I didn't know exactly what to expect. I thought that Marcel told me everything, all his hopes and dreams, fears and even mistakes, but there might be something inside the diary that would give me a clue.

The first entry was dated two years ago.

Man, this high school sucks. I wish I was in downtown Toronto or Montreal. Then I might feel more comfortable about being who I really am.

I remembered Marcel was deciding to "come out" at about this time. His friends and his mother knew that he was gay, but it was getting him down to have all these beautiful girls asking him out and to keep refusing or making up some excuse and then being forced to deal with their feeling of rejection. It was wearing him down. Eventually it came out that he was gay, and then he had to deal with the taunts of everyone who felt uncomfortable with his honesty. I flipped over a couple of pages.

I met someone at the Leprechaun last night. We just talked and talked. He's really into art and in fact he goes to OCAD and wanted to see my stuff. I don't want to get my hopes up because every time I think I've found some- one it all falls apart.

I remembered that relationship with Tyler. He was a nice guy, and gave us lots of advice about our work, tips about putting together our portfo- lios. The three of us would go to art exhibits and coffeehouses downtown. I always asked Jon to come along, but he always refused.

I turned over a couple pages.

What if I don't get into Art College? I'm no good. Why did I even think I could be an artist?

Self-doubt. We'd all gone through it. Then, two months ago:

What does Erin see in Jon? He's such a jerk to her. I've caught him staring at me a cou- ple times and it gives me the creeps. Like, what's his problem? He knows that I'm gay and that Erin and I are just buddies.

That entry didn't really surprise me. Then the last entry.

That red truck is following me again. Third time this week. Shows up in the weirdest places — outside school, at my house, at work. Maybe I'm just being paranoid. Maybe it's not the same truck, because I can't read the license plate. The driver wears dark glasses and a cap. No one I know. I think.

That was it. I'd have to take this to the police. Maybe that policewoman would find something useful. I looked at my watch. Six-ten. I'd do it tomorrow.

My stomach grumbled. Dinnertime. Tonight was Mom's night to cook. I could smell chicken and some enticing aromas coming from the kitchen. Mom was just setting the food out when I came into the room. She waved a white envelope in the air.

"This came in the mail today."

I knew even before opening the envelope that it was a Christmas card from Dad. He was early this year. I felt like tearing it up, burning it, anything to get rid of his pathetic gestures. Didn't he know that little cards and token appearances couldn't replace having a real dad? Of course he knew. He just didn't care.

I put the card away without opening it and cleared my head to enjoy my mom's great cooking.

Chapter 10

When Mom dropped me off at school on Monday, a couple of kids turned and stared at me. I heard one of them say, "There she is." I didn't have a clue what was going on. Then as I walked up the concrete stairs to the school, a guy from a crowd of smokers called out, "Gay freak!"

I turned and stared at him.

"You got a problem?" I tried to keep my voice steady, not revealing the fear I had inside. It was just me against this guy, but he had at least ten friends all staring at me.

"Yeah, I got a problem with gays and an even bigger problem with people pushing their agendas down my throat."

Now I was really lost. I didn't even know this guy. How could I possibly be pushing my agenda down his throat? My look of confusion must have registered with him. He spat on the ground before saying, "Who do you think you are, writing to the paper and stuff? Criticizing people who aren't artsy brainers like you?"

My mouth dropped open. My article must have been published in one of the newspapers. I wanted to ask him where he'd read it, but I figured my enthusiasm would stir up more negativity. He turned back to the rest of the group, all huddled together smoking.

I'd have to find out. Go to a convenience store at lunch. I didn't have time now. I glanced at my watch. Eight-forty-five. Shit, I was going to be late. I rushed to my locker, threw in my bag, grabbed my English books, and headed to class — but not before I heard Amy's high-pitched voice call to me.

"Erin! I'm so proud."

I turned. She had a stack of newspapers in her arms.

"Which one published it?" I asked, trying to keep my voice low so as not to attract unnecessary attention, but people still stared at us. Amy's enthusiasm wasn't helping any.

"All three. Look!" She started to open the *Star* and the rest of the papers fell to the ground. It was crowded and kids were rushing to class. No one stopped to help. Instead, seeing the opportunity to create chaos, a couple of kids started kicking the newpapers so that they flew open and loose pages flew everywhere.

"Hey, don't be a jerk," I said to one guy as I tried to collect the flying papers. Amy just stood there, looking like she was going to cry. She held the *Star*'s editorial page open.

"Sorry, Erin," she said, looking at the mess on the floor. By now there was paper everywhere.

"Hey, what's going on?" It was one of the VPs. When kids heard his voice, they began to move off quickly. "That's enough. Get to class."

"I'm sorry, Mr. McGelegi," Amy started.

He looked like he was going to explode. His face was red and he had that I'm-counting-to-ten-before-saying-anything look plastered across it. "Just get to class. I'll have a custodian clean this up." Then he stormed off, muttering under his breath, "Great start to my day."

"Man, that's a guy who loves his job," I said, grabbing Amy by the arm and steering her to home-room. I hated standing in the hall for "O Canada" and announcements. We walked in the room just as the second bell rang. Mr. Galaghan looked like he was going to say something, give the usual spiel about being late, but he just waved us to our desks. As I stood at attention, I glanced at his desk and saw the three papers. God, how did everyone in the world know my letter had gotten published but me?

Mr. Galaghan took his time about taking atten-dance, reading the announcements, and handing out slips for detentions or guidance appointments. Then he paused, picked up the papers, and walked to the front of the class. He placed the newspapers on the desk in front of him and looked at me.

"One of your fellow students has had the privilege of being published in three of Toronto's daily papers. Erin, would you like to read your letter to the editor to the class?"

"Not really," I said, knowing my face was turning red.

"Do you mind if I read it to the class?"

I shrugged, then put my head down on the desk. It seemed to take forever for him to finish reading. When he was finally done, the class clapped. That just made me more embarrassed.

"What I want to point out, Class, is Erin's perfect argumentative essay style." He then went on to use my essay as an example of proper essay structure: opening paragraph statement followed by example, next statements followed by more supporting evidence, and a clear conclusion that tied nicely back to the introduction. He was getting right into it, but looked at the clock. Five minutes until the end of class.

"That's enough for today. Homework tonight is to read the essay 'A Room of One's Own,' then answer the question on page 245 and write a two-page essay on one of the choices from page 259."

The class groaned. Then the bell rang.

It felt really weird walking down the school hall and having people stare at me. A guy from one group called out, "Hey, Ms. Journalism, want to write a story about me next week?"

It was on the tip of my tongue to say, "Yeah, and I'll entitle it 'The Jock Without a Brain,'" but I held my tongue.

In French class, Madame Lachance must not have heard about my letter-writing feat or, if she had, she wasn't interested in talking about it. Instead she asked me, "Comment est Marcel?"

"La même," I responded, *the same*.

"C'est dommage." She shook her head.

We quickly dove into our assigned chapter of *L'étranger*. I loved this class — the comfort of the language, the familiarity of thought and expression. It was like being at home, being in my own culture, amidst my own words and philosophies that made me feel comfortable and nourished. Art was great, my passion. But art was still hard work. Whenever I entered French class, especially this class, which was all on literature, I felt at home. While some of the other students felt that the works we were reading were too dark, too pessimistic, I felt a real connection to their thought and intent — in particular this work by Camus.

* * *

In art class Mr. McPhaden gave us a list of things that had to be done for the show at the Oshawa Art Gallery on Saturday. I'd almost forgotten about it. Marcel and I had been so excited about showing our work and getting it ready, but that was before the attack.

"Are you okay, Erin?" Amy asked, coming up from behind, carrying one of her finished paintings that needed framing.

"Yeah, yeah … It's just been a weird day. A bit overwhelming."

"You're lucky."

"How so?"

"You're good at so many things. Writing, French, art. If one area doesn't pan out, you can always specialize in something else."

"What are you talking about? All you need is your art. You've got what it takes."

"I used to think that, but Jesse and his family don't think that being an artist is a good career for a woman to pursue."

That did it. I slammed my hand against the table. "Oh, for God's sake, Amy! How can you listen to that half-wit? Why don't you just tell him to go back to the Middle Ages!"

Tears welled up in Amy's eyes. She took a couple of deep gulps. I felt rotten for exploding at her.

"I'm sorry, Ames, but sometimes I feel that guy is too controlling. Too rigid."

I walked over and gave her a hug. Her painting was between us.

Amy sniffled. "I wonder that myself at times."

A buzzer from the intercom sounded.

"Mr. McPhaden, is Erin Martin in class?"

"Yes, she is."

"Could she come to the office for a moment?"

The typical "Oh, Erin, what did you do wrong this time?" taunts followed me as I headed out the door to the office.

It was weird walking in the halls when nobody

was around. I almost felt like a criminal. It had been pounded into our heads — no students allowed in the hallways during classes — every day on announcements, as if we couldn't remember the rules.

When I walked into the office, my attention was immediately focused on a middle-aged woman who was yelling at Mr. McGelegi. "No one in this goddamn school is going to get away with messing with my kid."

Mr. McGelegi looked like he was ready to end this woman's ranting with a quick swat to the head. He was responding to her in a level monotone, apparently in a futile attempt to calm her down. "At Oshawa Secondary, we have a zero-tolerance policy for violence. Your son started the fight."

"There's no fucking way he did. You fucking teachers just want to blame everything on him, ruin his life."

"There is the major problem of him carrying a weapon."

The woman stood still for a second — gathering her thoughts, planning a retort. I was mesmerized by this exchange. The secretary must have been saying my name a few times, because she ended up speaking loudly enough that both Mr. McGelegi and the mother stopped and turned to look at her.

"Erin? There's a message for you."

The secretary held a pink slip of paper in her hand with the name Dorothy Blake, the phone number 439-5555, and the words *Call me as soon as possible.*

It took me a second to register who this was. Then it hit me — the cop on Marcel's case. Cool. Maybe she'd found some more leads; maybe they'd caught someone. In any case I wanted to give her Marcel's diary.

As I headed back to my classroom, I spotted a familiar black jacket sauntering up the hall ahead of me. My heart started to beat a million miles an hour.

"Hey!" I called in a loud whisper. He didn't hear and I was afraid of getting caught by a teacher, so I ran to catch up to him. "Hey, Jon," I said, just as I was almost behind him.

He wheeled around defensively, then relaxed when he saw it was me.

I wrapped my arms around him, snuggled into him and breathed the smell that was unique to him, that made me feel light and high.

"This is a nice coincidence," he said, bending to kiss the top of my head.

"Yeah." I raised my head and put my arms around his neck, giving him a huge kiss.

"Wow. Let's cut classes and go to my place. No one's home."

I was tempted, really tempted. I wanted to be close to him, feel his arms around me, hear his gentle words and soft caresses. It's what I wanted more than anything. But then I remembered art class and my work there and the message from Dorothy Blake.

"Can I take a rain check?" I said lightly, kissing

his neck and rubbing my head into his chest.

He pushed me away roughly. "What is it with you these days? You used to be fun. You used to be up to doing anything any time. Now you're a drag to be around."

That did it. I hated it when he was mad at me. Besides, I really did want to be with Jon. So even though I had tons to do, I gave in.

"Okay," I said. "I don't want to miss the chance to be alone with you."

He relaxed and smiled.

"Let's go," I said in a voice far cheerier than I felt.

Chapter 11

We walked out the side doors.

"Brrrrr, it's cold," I said, hugging myself, wishing I could have gone back to class to pick up my jacket — but I wasn't that dumb.

Jon removed his leather jacket and put it over my shoulders. His smell engulfed me. The warmth of his coat felt good and then he put his arm around me — pure heaven.

It was easy to forget art class, the exhibition and Marcel for the moment, when Jon was being nice like this.

The walk to his place was ten minutes. His family — mom, dad, and two sisters —lived in South Oshawa in what looked like a townhouse; it was really just six apartments together in a row. The house was empty as he had promised. The smell of stale smoke and cooking oil struck me as we walked in. I never really liked going to Jon's place — mostly because of his father, who was always drinking and was sometimes downright mean to Jon's mom.

As soon as the front door closed, Jon kissed me, held me close.

I pulled away, "Whew, you're the world's best kisser." Then I kissed him lightly on the neck and stroked his face trying to quiet things down a bit. I could tell he was disappointed, but my light kisses seemed to satisfy him.

"How about something to drink," I suggested. I was thinking about juice or water.

"That's my gal. Always coming up with the best ideas."

As he went into the kitchen, I walked into the living room and sunk into the squishy sofa facing a huge television.

Jon emerged from the kitchen with two beers. I shouldn't have been surprised. I didn't feel like drinking so early in the morning, but I didn't want to offend Jon by refusing so I put on a fake smile as he handed one to me.

"Thanks, honey."

He sank into the couch beside me and flipped the cap off his bottle, taking a huge slug. I opened mine as well. I usually preferred drinking out of a glass but, hey, I could handle drinking out of the bottle once in a while.

He reached for the remote. It was almost like an automatic reaction — sit down on the couch, turn on the television. He flipped through some channels as he continued to chug back his beer. At this time of day mostly talk shows were airing. He got bored quickly and finished his beer.

As he got up and headed to the kitchen, he asked over his shoulder, "Want another?"

"No, I'm okay."

He was back in a few seconds with another beer and something else in his hand — some cigarette papers and a bag full of weed. *Shit, he's not going to smoke up too*, I thought to myself, feeling a sense of dread.

But instead of opening his beer or rolling a joint, he turned to me and enveloped me in his arms.

"Hey, beautiful."

Then we kissed. We kissed a long time. It felt good. I felt wanted. Loved. Appreciated. As we kissed, I whispered, "I love you, Jon," and the way I felt at the moment *was* pure love.

Gradually, he started to touch me everywhere. I liked it, but I didn't want to go too far. I wasn't ready for sex. We had talked about this many times. I tried pushing his hands away gently, subtly. I didn't want him to feel rejected, but it was like his hands were magnets, always rushing back to the same parts of me. When he tried to unzip my jeans, I knew I had to say or do something more forceful. This was getting to be too much.

I pushed his hands away more assertively this time.

"Jon," I said in the most tender voice possible, "let's take a break. I'm thirsty," I lied, grabbing the beer and moving away at the same time.

"What's the matter with you?' he almost shouted. "You're such a bore."

I didn't want to get into an argument, so I just sat quietly.

He opened his second beer and practically drank the whole thing down in one gulp. Then he was up again and off to the kitchen. I could tell by his stiff shoulders that he was angry. I just hoped we wouldn't fight.

When he came back, he had two beers in his hand. He opened one and took a swig then reached for the bag and papers.

"Ah," he said, sniffing the contents of the bag. "Delicious."

Then he began the process of rolling a joint — something I'd watched him do many times. Usually I joined him for a few tokes. But I didn't want to do it this morning. I was starting to regret having skipped class and thinking about all the work I had to do to get ready for the exhibition. Not to mention Mr. McPhaden's disappointment that I had cut his class.

Thinking about the exhibition got me thinking about my new abstract — a painting Jon hadn't seen yet.

"Hey, I painted something pretty good last week. It's going into the exhibition," I said, trying to keep the conversation light.

He lit up his joint and took his first toke. He handed it to me, an invitation to join him. I shook my head to say no and continued to talk about the exhibition and all the work I had to do before Saturday. I knew I was rambling, but I was just trying to keep connected. He took a second toke and when he let it out, he exploded. "Will you just shut up? I could care less about your art. You know you're never going to be famous. Why don't you just quit while you're ahead?"

What he said made something in me snap. Why couldn't the guy I loved appreciate my passion? Then it hit me. If he hated art so much, why was he at the Gallery the other day? What was that all about? Before I could think about the consequences or how he'd react, the words were out of my mouth.

"If you hate art so much, what were you doing at the Gallery on Friday?"

He looked stunned for a second, almost wounded, like a little boy who's just been caught doing something naughty. But that look quickly turned to anger.

"I don't know what you're talking about. I don't do galleries. Remember?"

"Jon. I saw you in the nude exhibition looking at the statues." Then, as an afterthought, to hurt him like he was hurting me, I added, "The male nudes."

That did it. It was the final straw.

"You bitch!" he said, raising his arm to hit me, but I was alert, ready for it, and dodged the blow.

"I think it's time I leave."

"Yeah, get the fuck out of here," he shouted.

His words were slightly slurred from the beer and weed. I was glad. If he'd been more sober he might've kept at me until he finally hit me, just like his dad sometimes hit his mom.

I didn't have a coat to put on, so I rushed out the door into the chilly air. I started to cry. Running back to school where I should have been in the first place. Sobbing. Hating Jon for what he had just said and hating myself more for still loving him.

Chapter 12

"Erin! Great to see you!" Dorothy called across the room full of cops.

Heads turned and I momentarily thought about going home instead. I had come to the station straight after school, but I was beginning to think I was too tired to handle this.

Dorothy's desk was at the far corner of the room. The station was noisy. Telephones were ringing, photocopiers were running, people were talking loudly. I couldn't fathom how anyone could work productively in this environment.

As I reached Dorothy's desk, she stood up and reached out to shake my hand. I noticed then that she had copies of the newspapers on her desk.

"Have a seat," she said, pointing to the chair opposite her desk. "Great letter, by the way."

"Thanks" was all I could think of in reply.

"Due to your perseverance, they've put me back on the case."

Now she had my full attention. "I didn't know that you were off it."

She sighed and made a gesture as if to say, *look at this room*. "We are so busy, Erin, and like your article pointed out, Marcel's case was being overlooked because this is Oshawa. Stuff like this — and worse — happens all the time. We just don't have the person power to follow up."

I smiled at her politically correct version of "man power." Then I remembered the diary. "I almost forgot. Marcel's mom gave me his diary to see if there were any possible leads. I read through it and his last entry mentions something about a truck following him." I handed her the black book.

"This will be useful. Thanks, Erin."

"So do you have any more leads?" I asked, already knowing the answer.

"I'm working on it. What we have done is eliminate who it is not. It's not that neo-Nazi kid, although he says he wishes he'd done it, and it's not the goths. And none of the preps or jocks seem interested in the issue."

I nodded, urging her to continue.

"Did Marcel have any enemies that you know of? Anyone who'd want to hurt him this badly?"

I quickly went through the file of possibilities in my brain. Marcel didn't have a lot of friends. There was Tyler, but I knew that when the relationship ended, things between them had remained on good terms. I thought of Marcel's other friends.

I shook my head. "I don't think it would be

someone who knew Marcel very well."

"Why's that?"

"Because he's such a likeable guy."

"Then what about drugs?"

"No. Marcel has tried the usual stuff — you know, he smokes a joint once in a while, but he isn't a druggie."

"So he sometimes smokes a little weed?"

"Sure. Not a lot, but sometimes."

"Who sells him his marijuana?"

"I don't know." It was true. I didn't.

"Does Marcel know anyone who's in The Apocalypse? Do you think he buys his drugs from them?"

"The biker gang? God, no! He's not like that."

"Okay, okay. Just asking." Dorothy pored over her notes. "Okay. So then there's his lifestyle."

"Yeah," I said slowly, already knowing what she was hinting at.

"Oshawa isn't the sort of place that exactly has a thriving gay community. We've ruled out the possibility of the neo-Nazis and goths. Is there any other group at school that is blatantly against gays?"

I thought about it, my mind going back to all the times that Marcel had to suffer taunts in the halls from jocks or girls. I told Dorothy about the girls who were interested in Marcel and how they were sometimes insulted when he wouldn't go out with them.

"That's a start. Do you know their names?"

"Only one for sure. Michelle Seckler, who asked him to the prom last year."

"Were they friends?"

"Michelle and Marcel? No! She's a party girl. Not even the kind of person Marcel would hang out with."

"Do you think she might've been angry enough to get someone to do this?"

"I don't think so, but who knows?"

Then I thought back to Amy's comments about Jesse and his religious convictions. Would someone be so angry at a person whose beliefs were different that they'd beat that person up? Almost kill him? No, I thought to myself, that's barbaric — nobody in the twenty-first century could possibly be so dogmatic in their beliefs, so uncivilized, so intolerant. But then my mind flashed to September eleventh, and I realized that perhaps there were many people in this world I couldn't understand. And that, although it was beyond my comprehension that someone could behave in such a way — anything was possible.

"There is one person who really hated Marcel because he was gay," I started, tentatively.

She looked up from her notes and raised her eyebrows, encouraging me to continue.

"It might be totally out of line. I might be wrong."

"Go on."

"My best friend's boyfriend is Jesse Webber. He goes to this church, some evangelical, fundamentalist thing where they preach that homosexuals are despised by God and that gays should be punished. There's even some verse that Amy says points to the fact that homosexuals with AIDS are being judged by God."

Dorothy nodded her head. "It's more common than you'd realize. Did Jesse ever openly state that he wanted to hurt Marcel or someone else who's gay?"

"Not to me. I think he feels I'm part of the fallen many, that somehow contact with me would contaminate him."

"So, you've never actually heard him say that gays should be punished for their lifestyle?"

"Well, he did say something like that around me once. He said the attack was God's way of punishing Marcel for being gay. He's told Amy that lots of times. To such an extent that she's beginning to believe some of that garbage."

"Would Amy be willing to talk to me about things that Jesse has said to her?'

"Maybe if she knew it would help Marcel. But she's pretty tight with Jesse. I can't see her willingly getting him in trouble of any kind."

"So, let's recap. We've got the spurned lover possibility and the evangelical gay bashers. We've got the diary and his phone directory. It's something." Dorothy looked over her notes. "Oh, one last question. Does Marcel have any male friends who are blond?"

"Not that I can think of," I said finally. "Why do you ask?"

"Oh, just another lead, that's all." Dorothy smiled disarmingly.

"What else can I do?" I asked.

"You've been a great help, Erin, and I know it's probably affecting your schoolwork. So let me take over from here."

I thought of the art exhibition and how excited Marcel had been about having his work on display at the Oshawa Art Gallery. He had been practically bouncing out of his skin, but now he wasn't going to be around to enjoy the show. The thought of displaying my work without Marcel was pretty dismal. Dorothy must have noticed the sad look on my face.

"What is it, Erin?"

"Just thinking about this weekend. How Marcel had been looking forward to this art show for months. Usually it gets covered in the papers, and sometimes agents even stop by to check out the new talent."

"You can still take Marcel's work there for him, can't you?"

It was Monday. The show was on Saturday. I barely had time to get my own stuff framed and ready, let alone Marcel's, but I knew that Marcel would do the same for me.

"You're right."

"What time is the show?"

"Eleven until two."

"I might drop in. My son likes stuff like that. It would be a fun outing for him."

For a moment it jarred me, Dorothy mentioning her kid. In this office with her uniform on, she looked so cool and professional. I knew she must have a personal life, but I hadn't actually pictured her with a house and a kid.

"Yeah, well it's usually a half-decent show. Lots of my classmates are really good."

She stood up and I assumed that meant we were finished for the day. "Thanks for keeping me informed, Erin, and thanks for making the effort to write to the papers. Acts like that take a lot of energy and time, but they make the world a better place."

Now she was starting to embarrass me. I stood up and held out my hand across her desk.

"Could you let me know if anything comes up?"

"You know I will, Erin."

As I walked out of the building I looked at my watch. Four-thirty. There was still time to visit Marcel and Lucie at the hospital. When I had spoken to Lucie over the weekend, she had told me that Marcel seemed to be regaining consciousness. At least, the doctors thought he was improving. That was great news, and I wanted to see him for myself. But before I visited the hospital, I had to go to Bell Street. I was determined to see the place where Marcel was attacked. I wanted to see if there were any clues that the cops had missed, but mostly I wanted to see the site where someone had hated my friend so much that they had beaten him to a pulp.

Chapter 13

Bell Street wasn't hard to find. You just stayed on Simcoe and there it was, a little street running east off the main drag. I almost missed it in my determined walk. A tiny, nondescript sign indicated the location. There was a trophy store on the south corner, across from a lot overgrown with weeds, litter, paper, coffee cups, and bags. It looked quiet enough — even normal — certainly not what I would expect of the scene of a crime. The houses on both sides of the street were mostly little brick boxes. They seemed to be cut from the same pattern — large picture window and grey cement steps leading to a screened-in front door. Quiet. Boring. I could see the blue glow of televisions in some of the living rooms.

An older man was shovelling slush out of the gutter in front of his house. I was afraid to approach him, but knew that he might have some answers.

"Excuse me, sir."

He looked up, suspicious. His coat was a blue bomber jacket with a faded Toronto Maple Leafs insignia on the left-hand side.

I continued, despite his lack of encouragement.

"Is this the location where Marcel Lemieux was beaten?"

"Who's asking?"

"I'm his best friend and I just want to know."

"The cops have already been down here a couple times. But no one will talk."

"What do you mean?"

He nodded his head to the other side of the street where there was a large, rundown house with motorcycles parked in front of it. "No one's gonna mess with those guys."

"What guys are you talking about?"

He looked at me like I was from another planet. "The Apocalypse."

I tried not to gasp. "Do you think one of them did it?"

"Listen miss, I just mind my own business. I told the cops what I saw. There was some blond guy hassling your friend. That's all I know."

"Some blond guy?"

"Look. You want some good advice? Keep out of it."

He turned his back to me and continued his shovelling. It didn't take a brain surgeon to figure out that the conversation was over.

I glanced once again at the gang's clubhouse before my attention turned to a small apartment building standing next to it. On the third floor, a curtain pulled back and a woman's face looked out at me. I'd seen the woman somewhere before, but where? She looked at me as if she knew me and gave a little wave, then disappeared back inside. I turned to the man to ask him if he knew who she was, but his determined silence was not to be interfered with.

By now, it was late. I decided I would have to visit Marcel and Lucie another day. As I headed home, I pulled my coat tightly around me and dug my hands into my pockets. I felt the envelope before remembering — Dad's card. Shit. I wasn't going to let thoughts of him interfere, weave their way into my mind. I would chase them away, obliterate them as I had so successfully done all these years since he had left.

And yet the more I told myself not to think about him, the more I thought about him. I hated myself when I did that. It's like someone telling you not to think about pink elephants, then all you will think about will be pink elephants. The same was true about Dad. The more I tried to push the thoughts away, the more they came crashing in, flooding me, flooring me with their persistence. And I just couldn't stop the thoughts. Obsessive-compulsive behaviour was what it was called. "You're acting like a wingnut," was what Jon would say. I had to smile, he had the silliest way of calling me crazy, of helping me see that life wasn't as serious as I made it out to be. I liked him for that — not for calling me crazy of course, but for helping me not take myself so seriously.

When I got home, I had a voice-mail message from Amy, asking me to call her. I could tell she'd been crying.

She picked up on the first ring.

"What's the matter, Ames?"

"The whole world's falling apart."

"What happened?"

"Jesse just broke up with me."

Part of me wanted to shout, *Thank God*, but another part of me warned that I had to be sensitive to Amy and thoughtful about her feelings. "What did he say?"

"He said that I wasn't *really* a Christian and that he only wants to date *real* Christians."

"What does he mean by that? You're the most Christian person I know — kind, loving, forgiving. Isn't that what Christians are supposed to be?"

"According to Jesse, a Christian is someone who goes to his kind of church and believes his brand of Christianity."

"Amy, listen to yourself. That's absolutely crazy. How can there be just one kind of Christianity?"

"I don't know," she said, and she started to bawl.

"Do you want me to come over?"

"Not right now. Mom's taking me shopping. But can we get together tonight?"

"Sure."

"We've been meaning to watch that movie *Pollock*. Let's get that. Can I come over to your

place? It's just too noisy here with all the kids."
Amy had three younger siblings. Cute kids — a
twelve-year-old sister, a nine-year-old sister, and a
six-year-old brother. There was always something
fun happening at her house, which, I must admit,
I kind of missed in our quiet apartment, especially when Mom worked nights — but I don't think
I could have stood the chaos every day.

"Sure. No prob. So see you at seven?"

I shook my head as I dialled the Oshawa police
station. What a jerk that Jesse was! Who did he
think he was? The receptionist answered.

"May I speak to Dorothy Blake?"

I waited while they located her. Dorothy
seemed out of breath when she got to the phone.

I told her about what I'd learned about the site of
Marcel's beating. Yes, she was aware The Apocalypse had their hangout nearby. She was looking
into that. She also knew about the blond man who
was spotted with Marcel. She was looking into that,
as well. We chatted for a few minutes longer, and
then I hung up.

Six o'clock. Enough time to work on a painting. As I got my paints, brushes, and canvas ready,
I heard Mom's key in the door.

"Hi, Mom," I called out.

She stuck her head in my room and smiled
when she saw that I was painting.

"Good day?"

I gave her the highlights. "I hope you don't mind
that I invited Amy over tonight to watch a movie."

"You know that Amy's welcome here anytime. Pasta tonight."

She left and I could hear the pans and plates banging as she got dinner ready. I liked it when Mom was home. Just her sounds and presence made me feel comfy.

As I dipped my brush into the red oil paint, I thought about my fight with Jon and I wondered if he was still angry. My stomach churned at the thought. I would call him when I was done painting. I turned my attention back to the canvas and blotted out everything — Marcel, Jon, Amy, school. I focused on the colours, the swirl of the brush, the strokes against the canvas. Just when I was on the verge of losing myself in my painting, it came to me. The woman at the window — she was the waitress who had served me at the Gallery coffee shop. Bizarre. What did it mean?

Chapter 14

Waiting for Amy after dinner, I flipped through the application package for the Ontario College of Art and Design. I'd read this material over at least a hundred times — Admission Policies and Procedures. I had to have an Ontario Secondary School Diploma with thirty credits and a minimum of seventy per cent in OAC English — check. No problem in that area. Then there was the Portfolio Interview:

> An interview with each potential candidate will take place to determine whether a student will benefit from the type of education available at the college. The portfolio should include fifteen pieces of original work.

I jumped off the bed and flipped through the best pieces in my portfolio. An oil painting in reds and blues would definitely be one of the fifteen.

My watercolour of the ravine — another definite. A pen-and-ink portrait of my mom. I set that in front of me. I really liked it. Something about it captured the essence of my mom — the hope and sadness in her eyes. And then my thoughts turned to Dad. Dad who had caused the sadness. It made me churn inside thinking about him, and then for some reason my mind wandered to Jon.

Something wasn't right. I couldn't explain it exactly, but Jon was acting weirder than usual — more defensive, as if he were hiding something. Then a sick feeling came over me as I thought that maybe he viewed our fight as breaking up. Maybe he had already met someone else. The thought made me feel physically ill. I decided I had to call him. As I waited for him to pick up, I started doodling abstract line and dots. Then I heard his sister's voice.

"May I speak with Jon?" I asked.

"He's out."

His older sister Jenny and I weren't on the best of terms at the best of times.

"Do you know when he'll be in?"

"Late."

I continued to doodle. "If he gets in before eleven, could you have him call me?"

"Who should I say is calling?"

I knew she was playing this game just to bug me. It had happened so many times before. "Erin."

"Uh, okay."

But I knew he'd never get the message. "Thanks. Bye."

As I looked down at my doodle pad, the lines and dots were abstract, but the shape of a human body was clearly visible — a gaping wounded chest with a heart exposed and blood spurting out. It reminded me of a painting by de Kooning. Not bad for a doodle.

The doorbell rang. Amy had arrived. The first thing I did was give her a big hug. "How are ya doing, kiddo?"

"I'm okay."

I held her at arm's length and looked into her eyes. They were bloodshot, yet bright. She actually did look okay.

"Come in. Have a seat."

We walked to the couch and sank into the well-worn cushions.

"Do you want to talk about it?" I asked, knowing that Amy liked to analyze everything.

"He's such a jerk. I don't know what I ever saw in him."

I didn't want to agree too wholeheartedly, just in case they got back together. Criticizing your best friend's boyfriend often has a way of getting back to him.

So I was content to be there for her. "Do you think you'll get back together?"

"No! Not in a million years. You know I cried for a bit after we talked. Then Mom and I went shopping and when I came home I painted, and while I was painting it was like this huge load lifted off my shoulders."

"What do you mean?"

"Well, I was feeling so much pressure to be a certain kind of person when I was with Jesse. To believe all the same things that he believed. And I thought I loved him so I wanted to try to fit in with his church and his family."

"Do you think you actually loved him?"

"As I was painting I realized that it was more infatuation. I admired his religious convictions and his ability to speak his mind. Of course, there were also his looks."

I smiled.

"I'm glad that I got to know him and to understand his religion," she continued. "You know, Erin, it's really scary that people still believe those things."

I thought back to my conversation with Dorothy. "Do you think that Jesse or any members of his church would hate someone enough to beat him up because they didn't agree with that person's lifestyle?"

"You're talking about Marcel."

I nodded.

"Well, they're certainly against gays. There's no question about that. But to do something violent — I think that they would feel that that was wrong as well."

I told Amy about my conversation with Dorothy. "Would you be willing to talk to her? Tell her the things you heard during the sermons and when you were around his family?"

97

"I don't know, Erin. That's sort of speculative."

"It might solve the case on Marcel."

"Okay. For Marcel. How is he doing, anyway?"

"I didn't tell you! I talked to Lucie yesterday. He's coming out of the coma."

"That is so great! Is he talking about who did it?"

"They don't think he's ready to be pushed yet. They want to give him a couple of days before they put any pressure on him to remember stuff."

"Well, when he starts to talk, he might know the answer himself."

"Yeah, maybe," I said, and had this sick feeling in my stomach I couldn't understand or identify, like I was almost afraid for Marcel to tell us what he knew.

I pushed the thought out of my mind. "Let's watch the movie."

I popped the video into the machine and soon we were immersed in the world of painter Jackson Pollock — his life, his work, his rise to fame, his famous spattered canvases. We followed the film as it showed us Pollock's world, his dedication and his concentration. I was fascinated by his technique — the spattered paintings, "drippings" as they were referred to. His total abandonment to the act of painting, how he threw his body into the brush strokes — the spontaneity, the automatic responses. There wasn't enough actual discussion of his work. The movie focused more on his personal life — his relationships with his friends and colleagues and his wife. We learned about his alcoholism and his abusiveness. That sick feeling started to creep back in. Pollock was a genius, and yet he was horrible to his wife.

I guess it's hard to make a movie about a visual artist or a writer actually doing their work — then it becomes a documentary. Especially with Pollock's work the paintings can't even really be discussed because they are purposely not about anything. They are devoid of subject matter. As much as I love Pollock's work, the more I watched him get drunk, the more he yelled at his wife and cheated on her and made her life a living hell, the more I hated the man — not the artist, but the human being. As much as I tried to push it out of my mind, tried to ignore the facts that were pounding their way into my psyche, I couldn't help making a comparison between Pollock's behaviour and Jon's.

It was true that Jon had never hit me, but during our last fight he had tried. And the way he put me down, his distance, his discouraging comments about my work; the way he never complimented me; how he diminished everything about me — suddenly all these things seemed obvious. How could I have blocked them out for so long? Our relationship wasn't healthy. Not for me, anyway. That was what Mom had been trying to point out, but I wouldn't listen.

As I watched the scenes of Pollock with his wife, I knew that I had to do something, something more than just talk to Jon about how I wanted to be treated, more than just beg for approval, approval that he seemed to purposely withhold. How do I look? What do you think about this painting? His responses were almost always put-downs, bored and dismissive.

The movie made it so clear to me. Jon's constant criticism had nothing to do with me and my not being good enough, as I had started to believe. Jon's inability to compliment me had to do with his own feelings of inadequacy, his own feelings of inferiority, even though he put on this cavalier front of not caring about what people thought. The person I had initially fallen in love with wasn't the person I had hoped he would be, the man I was hoping would fill the void left by my father. I now realized that it was all a huge farce. This realization struck me hard. I don't remember the last twenty minutes of the movie because I was off in my own world, thinking and thinking and then knowing what I had to do.

When the movie ended, Amy turned to me. "That was great!" she said enthusiastically.

But her tone quickly changed to surprise when she saw I was crying. "Erin! What's the matter? Did the movie make you sad?"

I nodded, then shook my head. I didn't feel capable of talking without bawling my head off. She put her arm around my shoulder.

"What is it, Erin? Tell me."

I took several deep breaths before I could finally blurt out, "I need to break up with Jon."

Now it was her turn to be quiet, to not comment. I knew she disliked Jon even more than I had disliked Jesse. She treaded cautiously in her next comments.

"What's wrong? Why now — after six months?"

"I just know."

And then I was gulping. Trying to keep my voice even. "I just realized that if I stay with Jon he would end up treating me like Pollock treated his wife."

She gave me a big hug. "How are you going to tell him?"

"I don't know. Whenever I try to talk to him about something difficult, he gets me all mixed up. Throws me off from my main point. Confuses me."

"Maybe a letter would be best."

"I think you're right. And I think I'd better do it before I lose my courage. Before I'm willing to stay with him a minute longer, settling for his crap."

"Do you want me to help you?"

"No. It's something I have to do myself."

"Do you want me to leave?"

"If you don't mind."

We hugged, and then she slipped out. Even before Amy closed the door behind her, I had begun the letter.

Dear Jon ... Then I stopped. Should I go into a long explanation of the reasons I was ending the relationship? No. Keep it simple.

I don't want to go out with you anymore. I don't love you anymore.

I scratched that last line out. It wasn't true. I did

still love him, but I couldn't tell him that or I'd just get sucked back in. I crunched up the paper and started again.

Jon, I don't want to go out with you anymore. I hope that we can still be friends. Erin.

There. Short and to the point.

I put the sheet in an envelope and threw on my coat and boots. Even though it was midnight, I had to deliver the letter before I changed my mind. Mom's bedroom light was out. I hoped she was asleep and wouldn't hear the apartment door close. The walk to Jon's house seemed to take forever, and the cold wind and darkness were unnerving. I kept looking over my shoulder to see if there was anyone behind me. It was almost enough to make me want to run back home and climb into my warm bed.

When I got to Jon's house, all the lights were out. I hesitated. My hand shook and hovered over the letter box. A moment of indecision. Could I live without him? Then action. I dropped the envelope in, turned around quickly and ran home, afraid to think about what I had just done and how Jon would react when he read it.

Chapter 15

The days leading up to the art show were a blur. Most of us were in procrastination mode and had to skip our other courses to complete our work. I talked to my English and French teachers; they weren't thrilled and made it quite clear that they would make no concessions or allowances for missed assignments.

It wouldn't have been so bad if I was just working on my own stuff, but I was also trying to pull together Marcel's. Some of his pieces could be mounted on laminate board, but other pieces needed framing. The woodworking classes were great — they put aside their other projects to help us make frames.

The only glitch in the week was Thursday, when the whole school was evacuated — apparently a package labelled "Anthrax" had been left in the girls' washroom. As we left the building, a team of cops in what looked like space suits, masks, and gloves were entering the building. I ended up going to the Gallery to see what I could do there about framing my work and Marcel's. Unfortunately, most of our art was still at the school.

Friday morning the radio station reported that the school was open and that the package had been bogus. So I was back in class — but how was I going to get all my work done?

"Are you okay, Erin?" Mr. McPhaden asked as I struggled to get my stuff done, downing coffee and chocolate in an attempt to stay alert.

"I'm fine. Just three more pieces."

"Can I do anything to help?"

"Well … could you help me with Marcel's work?"

"Sure."

So the seven of us, with Mr. McPhaden's help, scrambled to put the finishing touches on our own work as well as frame Marcel's — our eyes forever on the clock and eleven p.m. — the time when the school had to be locked up. At ten to eleven we finally finished. We were exhausted and ready for bed.

"I'll see you guys tomorrow. Seven o'clock. I'll load up the pieces in my van and meet you at the Gallery. All the work needs to be on the walls by ten. You guys are fantastic! Now go home and get a good night's rest."

Which, of course, was futile advice. I couldn't sleep a wink with all the thoughts roaring through my head. I couldn't stop thinking about Saturday's show. And then thoughts of Jon kept crashing in.

Why hadn't he at least called to bawl me out about my letter? What was he thinking? What was he doing? I hadn't seen him at school all week.

When I awoke on Saturday morning — I must have fallen asleep, after all — I felt butterflies dancing in my stomach. I was lightheaded, almost like I'd been drinking, but I hadn't had a drink in a week. Funny how, when I dedicated myself to something worthwhile, I didn't feel the necessity to obliterate the present or forget the past. I hoped that I could keep this up.

I smelled coffee and toast. I threw back the covers and grabbed a sweat top for over my pyjamas. Mom sat on the couch, curled up with a book and the cat on her lap. They looked so happy, so content.

I felt a sense of protectiveness toward my mom and went over and gave her a kiss on the cheek. She looked up, surprised, not used to outward demonstrations of affection from me since I was little.

"Coffee's ready and I made some French toast."

"Thanks, Mom."

Six-thirty. The show started at eleven. I wolfed down breakfast, the caffeine kicking me into high gear. I had already decided to wear my black dress pants, a black turtleneck and black blazer for the day. The buzzer rang.

"That's Amy," I called to Mom over my shoulder as I slipped on my jacket and backpack. I unlocked the dead bolt and chain and let myself out.

"I'll be there around noon, honey. I'm looking forward to it."

"See ya, Mom!"

Amy was waiting in the lobby. She had a canvas under her arm; it looked like a drawing.

"What's that?" I asked as I opened the door.

"A piece I drew last night. Couldn't sleep. Couldn't stop thinking so I just got up and drew."

"Are you going to put it in the show?"

"If Mr. McPhaden lets me. For sure. Do you want to see it?"

I didn't know what to expect, as Amy's subject matter ranged so drastically. But when I saw the picture of Jesse — well, parts of him — fragmented, divided in two, shades of black and white, I felt my throat go dry. Amy was back to her old self, creating brilliant, disturbing images, not pleasant ones.

"It's great, Ames. Do you think Jesse will have a problem with it?"

"Jesse couldn't care less about art, and besides he'd be flattered that I was still thinking about him."

"Are you still thinking about him?"

She gave me a sideways glance as if to ask, *are you kidding?*

"How many pieces do you have left to complete for your OCAD portfolio?" I asked her as we walked.

"Two more if McPhaden likes this one — sculpture and multimedia."

"You're way ahead of me. I've got four left."

"It's only November. You still have time."

"But you know me and procrastination."

"Hey, at least you're talking about school

again. For a while, I was afraid that you would chicken out."

"There's still time to chicken out."

"Yeah, but you won't." She gave me a punch on the arm as we pressed the buzzer and then waited for the caretaker to open the doors to the Oshawa Art Gallery. Everything was quiet, almost eerie. He showed us to a room toward the back of the building, the only place that was lit up.

When I walked in, I held my breath and stopped. Seeing our work propped up against the walls just blew me away. Everything still needed to be hung, but McPhaden had selected a place for everything. I walked around the exhibit slowly. I recognized my fellow students' paintings and sketches, but they seemed so different in this context. Amy walked right over to Mr. McPhaden to discuss her piece. I could tell by his expression that he liked it, and I could see that he was searching for a place to fit it in.

My abstract painting stood against a partition, the reds and blues appearing more vibrant in the light of the room. I stood for a moment looking at my work and seeing things that I didn't remember painting, an added dimension. Beside my abstract oil was Marcel's haunting watercolour. I wished that he could be here to share this moment with me.

Before I knew it, it was eleven o'clock. The exhibit was officially open. On the side table, crackers and cheese and sparkling grape juice were available. No one showed up for the first half-hour except the Gallery staff. I recognized the coffee-shop waitress and waved to her. She smiled back, but had a worried look on her face that made me uneasy.

By noon the room was packed with parents, friends, and relatives. I saw Dorothy and her son come in, and I waved to them across the room. Marcel's mom and mine arrived together, chatting in French. While I was talking to Mr. Galaghan, Dad came up and put his arm around my shoulder. I felt myself go stiff. Who invited him? Who the hell did he think he was, walking in like he was a normal father, there for me every day of the week? I squirmed out of his grasp.

"This is great!" he said, gesturing around the room, putting on his sincere act.

"Yeah. Thanks." Then, trying to make conversation, I asked, "So what's new?"

"Linda is pregnant." His happiness practically radiated off of him.

"Maybe you can get fatherhood right this time."

I turned away. I felt rotten. Rotten that he was here. Rotten that his new wife was pregnant. Rotten that I'd stooped so low to say what I'd said; to actually act like I cared.

At two, the crowd started to thin out. At two-thirty, Marcel's friend Tyler showed up. I gave him a big hug.

"Thanks for coming. Marcel would be thrilled to know you were here."

"I actually just came from the hospital. He's coming around — getting more lucid all the time, remembering more. There isn't going to be any long-term damage."

"Great. Has Marcel mentioned any names?"

Just as Tyler started to respond, there was a commotion in the front entry. Everyone turned toward the sound. Voices were shouting; something fell over with a crash; there was swearing. I thought I recognized a voice, and that voice was coming closer and closer to the exhibit room. Although drunk and slurred, it was unmistakably Jon's.

Jon staggered into the room like a bull in a china shop, rushing past the curator.

"Where's Erin?"

The curator tried to quiet him, soothe him. I could see another woman associated with the Gallery reaching for the phone.

I rushed over. "Jon, I'm so glad to see you," I lied, hoping to placate him.

"Right. That's why you dumped me. You stupid bitch!"

"Jon," I said trying to keep my voice level and low, "things were just not working out. Besides, I'm leaving for college in the fall. It's for the best."

"Art college! Talk about a waste of time!"

"Jon, you know I want to be a professional artist. I need the training."

"You'll never make it. You've got no talent. You're nothing without me!"

I felt my face redden as I searched for the right thing to say. At that moment, Tyler came over.

"Hey, Jon, maybe you should leave before the cops arrive."

"You stupid fag! Why don't you just shut up?" And before anyone could stop him, he punched Tyler in the face, knocking him down. Tyler lay there for a second, looking stunned, blood spurting from his nose.

Dorothy and two men grabbed Jon, restraining him.

"Fucking fags," he yelled. "They make me sick."

* * *

Eventually, the Oshawa police arrived.

When Jon saw the officers, he tried to shake off the two men who still had him by the arms. It happened so fast and yet in absolute slow motion. Jon fell backwards. Crashed. As he went down, so did the thin panel displaying my favourite oil painting. There was the sound of ripped canvas. The work was ruined. I felt sick.

As the police handcuffed Jon, I noticed the waitress from the coffee shop talking to Dorothy in a corner. I wondered what it was all about. I turned back to see what was going on with Jon and the police. The wind seemed to be knocked out of him. He had given up, like some wild animal that had been injected with a tranquilizer.

I walked to the entrance and watched the cops drive away. I didn't know whether I felt relief, anger, surprise, or sadness; perhaps what I felt was just a little bit of each.

Chapter 16

As soon as I got home, I flopped on the couch. I was exhausted. Mom was at the church, helping out with a dinner banquet. I wanted to sleep, but my mind wouldn't let me. It kept racing, thinking about Jon, thinking about all the hours I'd put into the painting that had been ruined, thinking about Dad. I wanted to push it all away and just remember the good parts of the day, but the bad parts kept swirling in my head, making me feel crazy.

The phone rang. It was Amy.

"How're you doing?" she asked.

"Oh, not bad considering I've just had my best painting ruined and watched my ex-boyfriend get hauled off to the police station."

She laughed at my sarcasm. "Want me to come over?"

"Actually, I'd love that. Mom's not here, and I'm feeling a little shaky."

"Who wouldn't after a day like today? I'll be

over in an hour."

Before I knew it I was sound asleep. I don't know how long I'd been sleeping when I awoke to a pounding noise. At first I thought I was dreaming, then I realized the sound was coming from the apartment door. I don't know why I opened it. Maybe I thought it was Amy, maybe I didn't take my usual precautions because I was half-asleep. But even if I had I checked the peephole, I don't know if I would have had the strength to tell him to go away, to keep the door closed. My emotions were still pretty mixed up. Whatever I may have been thinking, I wasn't prepared to see Jon.

As soon as I opened the door, he pushed by me, saying, "We've got to talk."

"Hey, sure." I tried to keep my voice light and wake up, get alert. But I was scared. I could tell we were headed for another fight. *Keep cool, keep calm*, I said to myself.

"So they let you off?" I asked, trying to keep the question light.

"Yeah, thanks to the old man bailing me out. But charges are pending. It's up to Tyler and the Gallery to decide if they're going to press charges."

"Oh …" I wasn't sure how to respond. I thought I'd try the tactic of being on his side.

"Maybe you'll get lucky and they'll drop the charges."

"Yeah, right. That's really likely with gay boy's friend and everybody else ganging up on me. I don't have a chance."

"You never know …" I was biding my time, trying to think of a way to get him out of the apartment, but my replies were getting weaker.

"Yeah, like you care. It's all your fault. This whole mess. First you and Marcel, then you dumping me. Why did you have to do that?" He swung around on me, his hands clenched in fists.

"Jon," I said, trying to keep my voice level, "you and I are so different."

"We used to like the same stuff."

"Yeah, but we're heading in totally different directions. I used to enjoy going out to clubs and getting high once in a while, but I want more out of life than that. I want to go to art school and make something out of myself."

"And I don't, right?"

"What colleges or universities have you applied to?" I asked, already knowing the answer.

"So what you are really saying is that you're better than me, right? Is that right?" He took a step toward me. "Maybe I should get them to fix you up the same way they fixed up gay boy."

My heart was pounding. "What are you talking about? Who are they?"

"I warned you to back off, didn't I? I left you a message in your locker, but you were determined to interfere. What did you tell that bitch from the cops?"

But before I could say anything, there was a knock on the door. Jon looked like he was going to order me not to answer it, but I was faster than him. "Come on in," I yelled. I knew I had left the door unlocked.

It was Amy.

She looked startled when she saw Jon.

"Hey, Jon. What's happening?"

"Jon just stopped by for a visit. We were just talking," I said in a tense voice. Amy looked at the two of us. Jon still had his fists clenched.

He glared at her. She looked at me. I mouthed the words, "Call the cops." I hoped she understood.

"I can't stay long, Erin. I just need to borrow your copy of *A Room of One's Own*. With everything going on this weekend, I forgot it at school and I haven't finished that assignment." Amy was lying, looking for a way to get out of the apartment.

Jon seemed to calm down in Amy's presence. He had a confused look on his face as if he didn't know what to do next. I quickly retrieved the book from my bedroom, hoping Amy could call the cops fast. As I handed her the book, I tried to relay this message with my eyes.

"See ya, Jon," Amy said in a tense voice as she left.

With Amy gone, Jon seemed to remember the point of his visit.

"So do you really want to know what happened to your buddy Marcel?"

"I know you never liked him."

"You got that right. I don't like customers who don't pay their bills."

Now I was confused. "What are you talking about?"

"Oh, come on, Erin. Don't play stupid. You knew he bought his stuff from me."

"Bought what?"

"Weed. God, you're dumb. How do you think I could afford that truck and all the dates I took you on? The jewelry I bought you for your birthday?"

He had moved in so close that I instinctively stepped back a pace and found myself against the wall. Now he pinned me there, his hands on my shoulders, his face inches away from mine. I felt lightheaded. What was he going to do? Then once again there was a pounding on the door and abruptly he let me go.

"Open up. It's the police."

Jon looked startled.

I kept my eyes on his face as I inched away from him toward the door. I'd read about boyfriends attacking their partners when they felt cornered, when they felt frightened, like a wild animal. They would lash out before they were caught.

I quickly opened up. Dorothy stood there, flanked by two cops.

"We're responding to a call about a domestic dispute. What seems to be the problem?" The officers stepped into the apartment.

I didn't want Jon to get into any more trouble than he already was in. I just wanted him to leave.

"We were just talking," Jon said, trying to keep his voice even.

"Is that true, Erin? Did Jon threaten you in any way?" Dorothy asked.

I looked at the floor, afraid to speak.

"I think I'd like to speak to Erin alone. Why don't we go out in the hall? You stay where you are, Jon."

Once we were outside, Dorothy closed the door behind us. Then she asked me the same question again. "Did Jon threaten you?"

This time I answered her. "Yeah, kind of." I told her everything that Jon had said and done including his mention of being involved with Marcel's beating. I kept my eyes glued to the floor as I talked. I didn't want to lose my nerve and back down.

When I had finished, Dorothy told me to stay outside and she went back into the apartment alone. A few minutes later, the two cops emerged with Jon handcuffed between them. They escorted him down the hall and out of the building.

Dorothy stayed behind.

"That took a lot of courage," she said, patting my arm. "You did the right thing."

All the pressures of the day crashed in on me, and I couldn't help it — I started sobbing like a baby.

I hadn't even seen Amy return, amidst all the commotion. She stepped over and gave me a big hug.

"Look," Dorothy said, "I have to go back to the station and try to piece all this together. We've laid charges against one of The Apocalypse—"

"You did?" I asked, interrupting her, "Why didn't you tell me?"

"It just happened today. I'll fill you in on all the details as soon as I can. I promise."

Once Dorothy was gone, Amy and I collapsed onto the sofa.

"I can't believe everything that's happened to you in just one day! I hope they nail Jon to the wall."

"I can't believe that I didn't see the real person for such a long time."

"Join the crowd."

"How could we both be so stupid?"

"Well, at least we'll be wiser next time."

"I don't think I'm going to be ready for a 'next time' for a long time," I said.

We sat quietly on the couch, each of us thinking our own thoughts, waiting for Dorothy to call and make sense of the mess.

Chapter 17

When the phone finally rang, it jolted both of us out of our reveries.

"Hello?"

"Erin?"

The voice was unmistakably Dorothy's.

I asked her the first question on my mind.

"What's going to happen to Jon? Was he involved with The Apocalypse?"

"Slow down, Erin, slow down. Let me start from the beginning. It was some members of The Apocalypse who beat Marcel."

"How did Jon get mixed up with those thugs?"

"Apparently Jon was getting his marijuana from the gang and selling it."

"Just to Marcel?"

"No. Jon had quite a few customers at your school."

"So what went wrong between Marcel and Jon?"

"Marcel apparently owed Jon some money. It

wasn't a lot, but Jon wasn't in the mood to be generous. The Apocalypse were coming down on him for money and I guess he decided to let Marcel take the rap. He told The Apocalypse it was Marcel's fault he couldn't pay up. They told him to bring Marcel down to Bell Street."

"But why such a vicious beating?"

"The bikers were just supposed to rough him up a bit, teach him a lesson. Jon says things got out of hand."

"How did you find out it was The Apocalypse in the first place?"

"Remember the woman I was talking to at the end of the art show?"

"Yeah. The waitress from the coffee shop."

"Well, she lives on Bell Street. She witnessed the attack."

It was then I twigged. I remembered the day I'd seen her watching me from the window of her apartment.

"Apparently she heard a ruckus around eleven that night. At first, she didn't think anything of it. Stuff like that is always happening around there."

"So what made her look out?"

"She heard a scream. Apparently that also isn't unusual for that neighbourhood, but after a while, she knew it was something more serious than just a couple of drunks taking shots at each other. That's what made her go to the window."

"She couldn't hear exactly what was being said. Something about Marcel paying up. We want to interview Marcel for his version, but it's too soon, I suspect.

"Anyway, when our informant looked out, she saw them kicking and punching Marcel. They just wouldn't stop. She's the one who called the cops and thank God she did or your friend might be dead today."

"So why didn't she come forward before?"

"Well, actually she did. She left us an anonymous message a day later, saying it was the bikers. She also gave us a pretty good description of the guy who did most of the dirty work. Big guy with a blond ponytail."

I remembered Dorothy asking me if Marcel had any male friends who were blond.

"Anyway, I guess she started to wonder what was happening so she came up to talk to me today at your show, and it all came out. She said that she'd met you in the coffee shop and was impressed with how important it was for you to find out who did it.

"It just worked out nicely that Jon chose to cause a public disturbance at that exact moment and then with what he revealed today we put the pieces together.

"I ought to get back to work, but I just wanted to let you know since you've been so involved and helpful. I'm sorry that you had to find out about Jon the hard way."

"I guess it's better now than later. But … it still hurts."

"I know. But believe me, you're better off without him."

"Thanks." One word didn't seem sufficient after all that had happened, all we'd been through, but it was the only thing I could say.

"Keep in touch, Erin. Tell me when you have your next show. My son really loved it."

"I will. Goodbye, Dorothy."

I hung up the phone carefully and fell back into the cushions of the couch. I couldn't believe everything that I had just heard. I was exhausted. All I wanted to do was go back to sleep. But Amy was waiting for an explanation and I owed her that.

So I proceeded to tell Amy all that Dorothy had told me.

"So it was The Apocalypse after all!" Amy said. "You know, you're not going to believe this, Erin, but I wondered if Jon might be involved."

"Really? We've been dating for six months. I thought I knew him."

"I don't know. There were times when he said some pretty nasty things to you, and I think he was jealous that you and Marcel were such close friends."

"You're right. I should've broken up with him a long time ago."

"So what do you think will happen to him?" Amy asked.

"I haven't a clue. I'm starving," I said, changing the subject, "Want something to eat?" I realized I hadn't eaten since that morning.

"Sure."

I went into the kitchen and came back with a bag of chips and some pop.

Amy still wanted to talk about Jon.

"What do you think Jon will get charged with?"

"I don't know. Dorothy didn't want to talk about it. Jon's never been charged with anything before although we both know he's done plenty he could be charged with."

"Yeah, that drinking and driving was starting to worry me. All those times you'd leave a club with him. I was scared. How are you feeling now?" Amy asked.

"Confused. Angry. Sad. Feeling like somehow I could've prevented the whole thing."

"Don't be ridiculous. How can you even imagine that?"

"If I'd been a better girlfriend or if I'd known about his involvement with The Apocalypse, maybe I could've helped him."

"Erin, you can't take the blame for Jon's actions! He's responsible for himself."

I knew Amy was right.

"How are things between you and Jesse?" I asked.

"He keeps calling, telling me that his parents made him break up with me. He wants to date secretly."

I snorted and rolled my eyes.

"Exactly," Amy continued. "I told him that if he wasn't strong enough at eighteen to make his own decisions, then he wasn't the right guy for me."

I took a sip of pop. "To tell you the truth, I never liked Jesse, but I didn't want to tell you because I thought you'd get mad at me."

"Yeah, I admit I was smitten. It was nice to feel loved. It's the little things I miss, like holding hands and the way he put his arm around me. I guess that stuff sort of blinded me about who he was at the core."

"I can relate to that."

"Besides, who needs men?"

We looked at each other and in unison said, "Us."

"But being single for a while won't kill us."

"That's for sure. Besides, now I'll have time to get my portfolio together."

"A lot of serious artists and writers and musicians are single."

"And we're going to be great."

"Better than great!" Amy said. And we gave each other a huge hug.